Praise for *The Dream Weaver*

"'Dreams need time and freedom to grow and change.' This is what stuck with me the most as I watched Zoey struggle to find her voice. Zoey is processing her own losses while trying to navigate her father's dreams, her brother's plans, and her grandfather's grief. My twelve-year-old self would have loved a friend like her. When one girl's voice gets louder, we all get stronger. Go, Zoey!"

—Doreen Cronin, *New York Times* bestselling author of *Cyclone*

"Brimming with heart and humor, Reina Luz Alegre's *The Dream Weaver* is a tender story about belonging, friendship, and finding the courage to fight for your dreams. Lovely and empowering."

—Ashley Herring Blake, author of the Stonewall Honor Book *Ivy Aberdeen's Letter to the World*

"A debut full of complicated families, complicated friendships, and the complicated and awkward experiences of growing up (including an embarrassing yet relatable first period experience that would have brought comfort to me during my own embarrassing early period days). *The Dream Weaver* is a story I would happily hand to all the middle grade readers I know. From one Jersey boardwalk kid to another, Zoey is the type of character I could have spent hours with at the shore."

—Nicole Melleby, author of *Hurricane Season*

"Charming, vivid, and emotionally real, Zoey's story will capture your heart! Deploying her can-do attitude and resourcefulness, Zoey discovers that her own dreams are worth striving for and that reconnecting with her past might be the best way to brighten her future. On the Jersey Shore, Zoey reawakens to her heritage and the memory of her mother, while also trying to make new friends. Past and future collide as her brother packs for college, her father takes a new job, and her grandfather's bowling alley drifts into decay. As Zoey tries to find her footing, she takes a risk on a project that could affect Poppy's bowling alley forever. Flavorful details, a quick-moving plot, and psychological depth bring this Cuban American family to life. A treasure for any library."

—Rebecca Balcárcel, author of Belpré Honor Book
The Other Half of Happy

"Zoey is a root-worthy character! She is the only girl in her family, the peacemaker between Poppy, José, and Dad. I loved reading along as she navigated weird new friend moments and embarrassing period happenings all in stride. This book has an endearing cast of characters from Zoey's older brother, José, who is not only full of perpetual optimism, but handles Zoey's first period with a chillness that is so refreshing and AWESOME! This story really encapsulates family and friendships—the good, the bad and the messy. It also reminds us that there are always good people willing to help us when we need it."

—Kristi Wientge, author of *Honeybees and Frenemies*

"A wonderful debut by Reina Luz Alegre! Told in clean and engaging prose, this story will thread readers through one girl's coming-of-age as she struggles to keep together her fragmented family, each holding their dreams close, while contending with a longing to connect to lost traditions without her mother, and finding what will make *her* feel truly at home. A heartwarming book about growing up, growing friendships, growing the bonds of family and culture, and growing dreams of your own."

—Aida Salazar, International Latino Book Award–winning
author of *The Moon Within*

THE DREAM WEAVER

REINA LUZ ALEGRE

Simon & Schuster Books for Young Readers

NEW YORK   LONDON   TORONTO   SYDNEY   NEW DELHI

SIMON & SCHUSTER BOOKS FOR YOUNG READERS
An imprint of Simon & Schuster Children's Publishing Division
1230 Avenue of the Americas, New York, New York 10020
This book is a work of fiction. Any references to historical events, real people,
or real places are used fictitiously. Other names, characters, places, and events are products
of the author's imagination, and any resemblance to actual events or places or persons,
living or dead, is entirely coincidental.
Text copyright © 2020 by Simon & Schuster, Inc.
Jacket illustration copyright © 2020 by Elizabeth Stuart
SIMON & SCHUSTER BOOKS FOR YOUNG READERS
is a trademark of Simon & Schuster, Inc.
For information about special discounts for bulk purchases, please contact
Simon & Schuster Special Sales at 1-866-506-1949 or
business@simonandschuster.com.
The Simon & Schuster Speakers Bureau can bring authors to your live event.
For more information or to book an event, contact the Simon & Schuster Speakers Bureau
at 1-866-248-3049 or visit our website at www.simonspeakers.com.
Jacket design by Lucy Ruth Cummins
Interior design by Hilary Zarycky
The text for this book was set in Adobe Caslon Pro.
Manufactured in the United States of America
0420 BVG
First Edition
2 4 6 8 10 9 7 5 3 1
Library of Congress Cataloging-in-Publication Data
Names: Alegre, Reina Luz, author.
Title: The dream weaver / Reina Luz Alegre.
Description: First edition. | New York : Simon & Schuster Books for Young Readers,
[2020] | Audience: Ages 8–12. | Audience: Grades 4–6. |
Summary: "Twelve-year-old Latinx Zoey navigates the tricky waters of friendship and
family while searching for a way to save her grandfather's bowling alley from closing"—
Provided by publisher.
Identifiers: LCCN 2019037535 (print) | LCCN 2019037536 (eBook) |
ISBN 9781534462311 (hardcover) | ISBN 9781534462335 (eBook)
Subjects: CYAC: Friendship—Fiction. | Family life—Fiction. | Cuban Americans—
Fiction. | Coming of age—Fiction.
Classification: LCC PZ7.1.A43435 Dr 2020 (print) | LCC PZ7.1.A43435 (ebook) |
DDC [Fic]—dc23
LC record available at https://lccn.loc.gov/2019037535
LC eBook record available at https://lccn.loc.gov/2019037536

Dedicated to my family

Zoey stared at the rows and rows of makeup in front of her. Glittery lip glosses to her left. At least a dozen different kinds of mascara to her right—all promising lush, full lashes. Above, rows of foundation compacts for a wide range of skin tones. And beneath, rainbows of shimmering eye shadow and bright nail polish, just begging to be browsed. But Zoey's hands stayed in the front pockets of her jeans. She'd watched so many tutorials online, and yet she always chickened out when it came to actually buying the stuff. It didn't help that Dad would say it was a waste of money, either. She knew Mami would probably say the same thing if she were here. From what Zoey could remember, Mami had rarely worn more than a touch of blush, a dab of lipstick.

But of course, her mami had been beautiful—she didn't need anything extra. Still, Zoey couldn't help craving a dramatic transformation for herself. And it was more than just makeup she wanted—all the other girls at school magically knew what patterned tops and colored bottoms paired well, and how to coordinate outfits with fun shoes and costume jewelry. Zoey looked down at her own T-shirt, denim shorts, and beat-up, faded flip-flops. She wouldn't even know where to start—and not knowing was embarrassing.

It reminded her of when she was little and Poppy had expected her to answer his questions in Spanish about school or the new toys he and Abuela had bought her. A language she *should* have spoken better—Mami had spoken almost exclusively to Zoey in Spanish before she'd started preschool years ago—but that left her feeling like a phony in her own skin.

She wished her mother were still alive so she could talk to her. But even if Mami were here, Zoey wasn't sure she could find the right words to describe this uneasy mess of feelings that sank along with all her other problems into the pit of her stomach.

"Zoey! Where are you?" A deep, urgent voice cut through Zoey's thoughts.

"Aisle nine!" Zoey called back.

A head of curly, dark hair poked around the aisle.

"Stop wandering off," José scolded, deftly maneuvering a cart between a baby stroller and a delicate display of perfumes.

"I'm twelve," Zoey said. "I don't need to hold your hand like a little kid."

"No, you need to help me find all the stuff on my list," José said. He glanced at the endless tubes of concealer and foundation. "I don't need anything from here. *Vamos.* Come on."

Sighing and rolling her eyes, Zoey grabbed the cart from him and turned it around.

"Hey there. Don't help me *con mala cara*," José chided. "Leave the attitude in the aisle."

"Sorry," Zoey said, meaning it. *Con mala cara* had been one of their mother's favorite phrases. It meant literally "with a bad face" and hearing it always made Zoey imagine evil fairy tale queens or cackling cartoon villains.

José looked down at his phone. "Okay, we've got the pillow, laundry bag, detergent, trash bags. . . . I still need bed sheets. I think they're that way."

Linens turned out to be on the other side of the store. Zoey's stomach hurt as they walked. A few days ago, a dull ache had started just below her belly button. It was right around the time she'd done the math and realized she had only six weeks left before José went away to college. It totally sucked. José wouldn't be here in August, helping Zoey buy supplies for her first day at yet another new school. Having José around always made settling into a new place easier. And this time was extra hard because they'd just moved in with their grandfather Poppy on the Jersey Shore, and Dad didn't exactly get along with him.

"Navy or green?" José asked, plucking the last boxes left under the cheapest price for twin XL jersey cotton.

Zoey shrugged.

"What's wrong? You're so quiet."

Zoey said nothing. She didn't want to make José feel guilty about leaving. But she didn't want to lie to him either.

"Tell me," José insisted.

"I don't want you to leave me," Zoey finally said in a small voice. To avoid José's gaze, she busied herself reorganizing the items in their shopping cart, making space for the set of sheets in José's hands. He tossed them in.

"Aw, Zo. It's going to be okay."

The dull ache suddenly turned into a sharp pain and Zoey bit her lip to keep from crying. She hoped José didn't notice and think she was being too emotional. But thankfully, he seemed oblivious.

"I *have* to go to college," José said, spreading his hands matter-of-factly. "I'm not doing it to leave you. If I

want to become an engineer, I have to learn how. College
has always been my dream. You know this."

He playfully elbowed her ribs. Zoey nodded reluc-
tantly, still fighting down the lump at the back of her
throat. She tried sucking in her stomach, which seemed
to help—but only slightly. Of course she knew her
brother's dream was to be an engineer. He liked science
and building solid things and math. Every decision was
carefully weighed and measured in José's world. But
Zoey suspected José hadn't assigned homesickness or
missing family much weight when he'd decided to go
to the University of Florida. After all, Dad made them
move so much that they didn't really have a permanent
home.

"I know. It's your dream. Like how Dad dreams of
owning a food truck on the Jersey Shore."

"Ugh. *Don't* compare me to Dad," José groaned,
pushing the cart toward the shower caddies. "I've wanted
to be an engineer since third grade. Dad's constantly
changing his mind."

"Dreams need time and freedom to grow and change,"
Zoey said automatically. It was what their father always
said. And at least Dad took them with him when his
dreams led him halfway across the country, unlike José.
For a second, she wished she could stow away in one of

José's duffel bags and go live in his dorm.

José's jaw twitched. He rolled his eyes. "Don't quote him, Zo."

"Why not?" Zoey demanded. The pain had gotten worse again and now there was pressure beneath her belly button too. It felt like her stomach was the dumpster at the end of a trash chute, filling up with gross, heavy garbage bags, except she hadn't even eaten much today. Why did she feel so awful?

"You have to know the way Dad does stuff isn't normal. Burning through Mami's life insurance money every time we move? Switching jobs five times a year? Quitting every single one of his business ideas because he's not a millionaire by the end of the week? Dad's so-called 'dreams'"—José made air quotes—"are unrealistic, and he gives up on them too easily."

"He just likes to have new things to look forward to. What's so wrong with trying to make life interesting?"

José crossed his arms over his chest, exasperated. "Dad could mix it up once in a while, not every two seconds. He's a loser—"

"He's not a loser!" Zoey cut José off. "He's doing his best. And he's all we have. His dreams make him happy. And we can't afford for him to get so unhappy that he gets sick and dies too," she said, her voice shaking slightly.

"*¡Cálmate!* Don't get all dramatic. You have me, too," José said, sighing and pulling Zoey in for a side hug. "I just don't want you to think bouncing around like Dad is okay. Someday you'll have to choose one thing and work hard for it, like me. I studied. I tutored seventh grade math on the weekends to save up. I *earned* scholarships. . . ."

Zoey pulled away. "At least I'm not going to miss you putting down Dad all the time," she muttered under her breath. José didn't seem to hear though. He was deep into his lecture and sounded like he was reading one of his college essays about perseverance in the face of adversity.

Zoey tuned him out. She'd heard this spiel from her brother before. And she hated it when José called her "dramatic," like she was blowing some silly thing out of proportion. Her concerns about Dad were real, and with good reason. Zoey remembered how pale and dull Dad's bright blue eyes had gone after their mother suddenly passed away five years ago. Sometimes he still got that look—randomly at the mall when they walked by one of Mami's favorite stores or after coming home from an awful day at work, grunting about an evil coworker or a new boss who knew less about customer service than he did. And it wasn't just Dad's eyes that went sad. His face and shoulders would droop too. Then he'd lock himself in his room to watch a sports channel, barely talking to Zoey or José. Sometimes for hours. Sometimes for weeks.

When he got into his funks, Zoey was always terrified that Dad might have a heart attack out of the blue, like Mami, or maybe just slowly waste away in front of his basketball game. And then what would she and José do? They'd be orphans. Would they have to go to foster care? Would a new family adopt them? Were they too old to be adopted? Zoey had heard once that babies got adopted more often than bigger kids.

So Zoey was always relieved when a shiny new dream put the twinkle back in Dad's eyes. Dad needed his dreams, and they needed Dad, so Zoey and José had to support Dad's dreams. Why was that so hard for José to understand? It seemed like the straightforward logic that was usually right up his alley.

Suddenly, all the muscles below Zoey's belly button seemed to tighten, the way her calf muscles cramped sometimes after she ran a mile in gym class. Zoey winced, doubling over the cart in pain.

José abruptly stopped mid-rant. "Zoey? Are you okay? What's wrong?" he asked, clearly alarmed.

"Ow, ow, ow," Zoey whimpered, resting her head on the green twin XL sheet set. "My stomach is killing me, and . . ." She trailed off as, all at once, the pressure and pain eased. Except Zoey was suddenly aware of a wet sensation between her legs, as if she'd peed her pants. *Oh no!*

"Zo? What is it?" José asked again.

"It feels wet down there," she whispered miserably.

"You probably just got your period," José said. He pulled out his phone. "I'll wait here while you go to the bathroom."

Zoey's eyes widened as her heartbeat sped up. She'd given up on experiencing this rite of passage. Already five-foot-four, she'd been filling out sports bras for a while. But since no period ever came she figured her body had just decided not to menstruate. The same way some people just couldn't roll their Rs. But now that *La Tia Rojita* (Mami had always cheerily rolled the R when referring to her own period as "The Little Red Aunt") had finally decided to visit, Zoey felt anything but relieved.

What should she do? Was there time to run back to Poppy's house? Had she already bled through her shorts? Zoey spun in a circle in the middle of the aisle like a dog chasing its tail, trying to see if there were any dark stains on her butt.

José raised his eyebrows. "What are you doing?"

Zoey didn't answer right away, but she stopped moving and hugged her arms to her chest.

"It's. My. First. Period," she said, panic seeping into

her voice. Her whole body suddenly felt too warm and she looked down at her flip-flops, on the verge of tears. "And. I. Don't. Know. What. To. Do."

"What? I thought we talked about this, like, two years ago," José said. He sounded annoyed, like he'd crossed Zoey's first period off some mental list a while back and preferred not to revisit the subject.

It was true they had talked about her period almost two years ago—after watching this awful cartoon in fifth grade that made puberty sound like the zombie apocalypse, Zoey had come home with Questions. And, for lack of better options, asked José and Dad to explain the logistics the video had left out. What a mistake that turned out to be! Dad had awkwardly compared *La Tia Rojita* to a "really private paper cut that bleeds like heck once a month," while José read her the Wikipedia summary on menstruation. And then one about elephant shrews, because, apparently, they menstruate too. But none of that seemed to have prepared Zoey because she was *freaking out* right now.

"Just because we *talked* about getting my period doesn't mean I actually *got* my period then!" Zoey gawked at her brother and began to hyperventilate.

José's expression softened. He put a hand on her shoulder.

"Okay, breathe," he said. "I'll go get you the, ah, the supplies you need, and then you'll go to the bathroom. Everything's going to be fine."

Zoey nodded, swallowing hard.

She forced herself to take deep breaths until she spotted José walking briskly back from the feminine hygiene aisle with a package cradled under his arm like a football.

"Got it," José said, tossing the package to her.

She took one look at it before staring back at him in horror.

"Tampons?"

She batted the package back at him like a volleyball. José caught it easily.

"What's wrong? Aren't these the same brand Mami used?" José looked confused.

"Yeah, but Mami's not here to show me how to put one in," Zoey hissed, missing her mother more than ever. She took another deep breath. "And they look like they're the size of crayons. What if it doesn't absorb enough? Or what if it gets, you know, *stuck*? Can't you just get me pads instead?"

José squinted at the lettering on the box, searching for instructions.

"They're specially designed to be absorbent enough to do the job and small enough to be comfortable. I really don't think these are that hard to use. You just put—"

"José!" Zoey shouted, then quickly lowered her volume when she saw a few people in the aisle glancing their way. *Ugh.* The last thing Zoey wanted was for strangers to hear her talking about her period. "I don't want you to *explain* this. Especially in public! Just please get me the pads, okay?" she asked, feeling wretched.

"Yeah, okay," José agreed, glancing around the crowded aisle. "I get what you mean."

He returned with the pads, and, feeling slightly calmer, Zoey headed to the women's restroom alone.

Inside the bathroom stall, she saw that a bright scarlet mark the size of a credit card stained her underwear, and there were red dime-shaped spots on her shorts, too. Should she take them off and wash them and her underwear before she put on the pad? But then she'd be standing in front of the sink naked from the waist down in a public bathroom.

That seemed like a really bad idea.

And she wasn't sure what to do with the pad, either. She'd unwrapped it, but did it matter which end went in the front? And there were flaps on the side that had already gotten stuck to the underside of the pad. Zoey didn't think that was supposed to happen. She wished desperately that she could ask Mami what to do, or even her abuela, but Abuela was gone too. And knowing she didn't have any female relatives to call hurt worse than cramps. Zoey was about to dissolve into a big, sobbing mess when the door creaked open.

Zoey heard footsteps. A splinter of hope cut through her misery. Maybe the lady who'd just walked in was a store employee, or even a mom with kids around Zoey's age who wouldn't mind reviewing a few basics woman-to-woman.

"Um, excuse me," Zoey called from inside her stall, pulling up her underwear and shorts. "I, uh, I just got my first period, and I don't know what to do. Could you please help me?"

Zoey unlocked the stall door. But the person staring curiously back at her in the mirror over the sinks was no friendly mom or cashier. She was a girl around Zoey's age. And she was rocking the best cosmetics aisle nine had to offer. Sparkly blue nail polish. Matching sky blue eye shadow. False eyelashes or killer mascara. Purple highlights in her hair. Indigo fit-and-flare dress patterned in daisies. Zoey's cheeks flushed in humiliation.

"It's okay. I know what to do," Fashion Girl said confidently. "Do you need a tampon?"

"No, uh," Zoey mumbled, glancing down at the pad in her hand. "I have a pad. But um, there's blood on my underwear and shorts. And I was just wondering if I should clean it off first. But then, like, if I do that, my clothes will be wet and gross. . . ." She trailed off as Fashion Girl looked Zoey carefully up and down. Zoey felt even more self-conscious in her old, faded outfit.

"That shirt is pretty long," Fashion Girl said finally, still staring at Zoey's midsection. "It goes almost all the way down to your knees, so I don't think you need to worry about anyone seeing the stains on your shorts."

Phew. Zoey felt better—until Fashion Girl pursed her lips, appraising Zoey again in a way that made her glance down to make sure a river of blood hadn't just gushed down her leg.

"Actually, can you turn around for a second? Just do a quick spin?"

Zoey turned in a slow circle.

"Okay good, the blood didn't get on your shirt." Fashion Girl grinned. "So, if I was you, I'd just wipe my shorts and underwear in the stall with a dry paper towel or some toilet paper, put on the pad, and then wait to throw everything in the washing machine at home."

Fashion Girl waved a hand under the automatic paper towel dispenser and held out a couple of sheets. Zoey felt like an idiot for not thinking of this obvious solution on her own, but she gratefully accepted the paper towels.

Fashion Girl smiled again. The purple and blue rubber bands on her braces matched her outfit.

"Do you know how to put that on?" she asked.

Zoey looked down at the unwrapped pad in her hand.

"I mean, like, I know the sticky side is the one that goes on the underwear. But does it matter which part goes in the front?"

"I don't think so. If you fold it in half, the pad is pretty symmetrical," Fashion Girl said, sounding pensive.

"When I took off the adhesive strip the wings got stuck to the bottom. Does that matter?" asked Zoey.

"Nah," Fashion Girl said. "Not unless you have such a heavy flow that you really need the wings to hold the pad exactly in place to prevent a leak. But I didn't need the wings the first time I got mine." She shrugged.

"Okay," said Zoey, feeling slightly better.

"Go put it on and I'll wait out here in case you have other questions."

Zoey went back in the stall and stuck the pad to her underwear. It wasn't that complicated, really, she thought as she pulled up her pants. But then a new fear struck. Would everyone be able to see the outline of her pad through the denim of her shorts? Did she look like she was wearing a bulky diaper? You could always tell babies were wearing puffy diapers beneath their onesies. Zoey stepped out of the stall.

"Better?" Fashion Girl asked. Zoey avoided eye contact in the mirror.

"Sort of. . . ." Zoey hesitated, then figured if she'd asked this many awkward questions already, she may as well ask a few more. "Can you tell I'm wearing a pad? I feel like it's showing through my clothes, and everyone will be able to tell I have my period."

"I know! I felt that way too when I first got my period," Fashion Girl said sympathetically. "But no one can tell. Believe me. I used pads the first six months before switching to tampons, and no one could ever tell I was wearing one. But if you want, lift up your long shirt a little and spin around again, and I'll tell you if I can see anything on your shorts."

Holding her breath, Zoey did as directed under Fashion Girl's appraising stare.

"Didn't see anything," she said finally, with the same authority as a doctor delivering a favorable diagnosis.

Zoey exhaled and stretched her shirt down as far as it would go.

"Do you have any other questions?" Fashion Girl asked gently.

"No, I'm good. Thank you though. For everything,"

Zoey said, quickly washing her hands and drying them on the hem of her shirt.

"Happy I could help," Fashion Girl chirped, flashing Zoey one last grin before stepping past her into the empty stall. "Sorry, I really need to pee."

"Oh yeah. Sorry to make you hold it so long. Thanks again for explaining everything!" Zoey said. She wished again that Mami was still alive and had been the one to walk her through *La Tia Rojita*'s first visit.

Faster than she'd ever hustled down a soccer field, Zoey sped out of the bathroom. She nearly knocked over José, who stood leaning against the wall, playing a game on his phone and whistling along to the game's cheesy theme song. The opened box of pads sat at the top of the pile in the cart in front of him, pointedly waiting for them to pay.

"Are you okay, Zo?" José asked. "You were in there for twenty minutes. I was starting to wonder if you needed me to go in there to help—"

"I'm okay," Zoey said quickly, brushing past him, heading toward the opposite side of the store. She wanted to put as much distance between herself and Fashion Girl as possible. She had been nice, but she probably secretly thought Zoey was a total freak.

"Chocolate helps with cramps, right?" José asked.

Zoey paused long enough to look over her shoulder. "I think so, but my cramps aren't *that* bad."

"I have sympathy cramps. You're going to have to share some candy with me." José grinned, turning down the snack foods aisle.

Zoey laughed, feeling a hundred times better than she had all day. She followed him and waited while he grabbed a humongous bag of miniature assorted chocolates that included Snickers, her favorite. The bag was so big it could have fed at least three hours worth of trick-or-treaters on Halloween.

"All right," José said, glancing inside the cart. "Pads? Check. Chocolate? Check. You're all set, Zo. Now let's go get a dry erase board to put on my door so people in my dorm can leave me notes," José said, sounding excited.

The pain in Zoey's stomach returned. Only this time, she knew, it wasn't a period cramp.

2

"D id you buy the whole store?" Dad demanded back at Poppy's house.

He sounded mad as he untangled Zoey from the seven heavy bags she'd threaded her arms through. José's shoulders tensed, and he glared at Dad as he put his own bags down on Poppy's old brown couch.

"The only things we bought that weren't on my college list were chocolate and pads." José crossed his arms over his chest.

"But you already have elbow and knee pads for your skateboard. We don't have money to throw away on extras. You're going to have to return those."

José rolled his eyes. "We bought *menstrual* pads, Dad. Zo got her first period."

"José! You don't have to go around telling everyone I got my first period!" Zoey protested.

She glanced at Dad, who looked as uncomfortable as Zoey felt. "I thought you got your, *you know*, two years ago," he said.

"Um, no. I didn't," Zoey said quietly.

"Oh, uh, okay. . . ." Dad trailed off like he was trying to think of what else to say.

Silence swallowed Poppy's living room. Zoey wished she could step backward and disappear into the portrait of her six-year-old self, laughing down at them from its perch above Poppy's television. That girl, missing two front teeth, didn't need to deal with *La Tia Rojita* and all the awkward conversations she brought with her. Dad cleared his throat at last and raised his hands questioningly. "Congrats, I guess. On Auntie Red arriving for a visit. Wasn't that what your mom always called her?"

"Her?" José rolled his eyes. "Menstruation isn't a person. It's a biological process—"

"Thanks, Dad!" Zoey quickly cut in, massaging her wrists where the plastic bag handles had dug in and left marks. She glanced wildly around the empty living room, desperate to find a change of subject. The last thing she wanted was to listen to her father and brother bicker about *her* period. Talk about awkward. Her eyes landed on a black-and-white photo of Poppy as a teenager, leaning against a humongous antique-looking car, from when he stilled lived in Cuba.

"Is Poppy home?" she asked.

"No, he went to work at the bowling alley," Dad said, also sounding relieved to be moving on.

He turned back to José, and Zoey noticed how Dad stood up straighter to emphasize the inch and a half he had over him. *Oh no.* Dad always did that whenever he was about to lay into José.

"José, I want a straight answer. Where did you get the money to buy all this stuff? I hope you didn't hit up your grandfather for cash."

José's nostrils flared and his mouth twitched, just as Zoey knew they would. She'd seen Poppy slip her brother a few twenties over breakfast earlier that morning while Dad went to the supermarket. But José hadn't asked for the money. Poppy had just given it to him.

"José used the money he saved up working after school," Zoey interjected before José could answer. She made eye contact with her brother, and silently begged him to keep his mouth shut.

"Oh," Dad said, relaxing slightly as his eyes roved over the bags once more. "This is a lot though. How'd you afford everything?"

"There were, like, *tons* of sales. All the school stuff

was fifty percent off." Zoey beamed like they'd just won first place in a contest for Best Bargain Shoppers in the Universe. José said nothing and even managed not to roll his eyes again.

"Okay, well, that's great then," Dad said, exhaling and running his fingers through his dark, curly hair. He glanced at the front door, then leaned in to whisper as if he was afraid Poppy might be able to hear him all the way from his bowling alley eight blocks away on the boardwalk.

"Look guys, don't repeat this, but your grandfather's got some money problems, and we don't want to impose more than we already are by staying here. Do you understand?"

"Yup." José grabbed a couple of bags and huffed up the stairs to his room.

Dad gawked after him. "What's his problem?"

Zoey shrugged at Dad. "I have cramps. I need to find my pads," she said, hoping more talk about her period would finally make Dad end this conversation.

It worked.

"Ah, feel better, kiddo. I've got a couple of business meetings this afternoon. You'll be okay without me, right?" Dad asked, already beginning to walk away.

"Yeah, I'll be okay," she said, unearthing her pads

and a handful of mini chocolate bars. "Just going to run upstairs to change and then head out to keep Poppy company at the bowling alley."

Dad nodded before disappearing into the nook beside the stairs that Poppy used as a makeshift home office.

Still feeling stressed from her ordeal at the store and all the tension in their small house, Zoey eagerly retreated to the privacy of Mami's old room. She rummaged through the shirts and shorts she'd unpacked into her mother's childhood dresser. How Zoey wished her grandparents had kept Mami's old clothes for her! Leggings and leg warmers in every color of the rainbow. Cropped jackets. Oversized, off-the-shoulder metallic tops. Parachute pants. Black, lacy, fingerless gloves. Poufy miniskirts. Earrings that could double as bangle bracelets. The old Polaroids still taped to the dresser's mirror attested that seventh-grade Jasmeen had, indeed, been fabulous.

Finally selecting her comfiest soccer jersey and drawstring shorts, Zoey put them on and flopped back onto the bed, letting out a sigh of relief. Dealing with Dad and José reminded Zoey more and more of living with a bad cough. The negative energy between them was like a persistent tickle at the back of her throat that could develop into a full-on attack at any time. Zoey had learned to stave off big fights between her father and brother the same way someone might eat honey or avoid talking too much to hold a cough at bay. Sweetly distract José with a tough question. Ask Dad about how work was going. Be as quiet and independent as possible, so as not to bother either of them. But it was an imperfect science and Zoey often found it exhausting to live as if she were walking on eggshells around both of them. Sometimes she just longed for peace and harmony at home that didn't require her to strategically manage her family's moods.

She scrolled through her phone for a while, looking up suggested remedies for cramps. She decided she would try warm compresses later. But for now, Advil sounded like a good idea. José kept the medicine in his room. When she came to the door, he stopped reading the book he'd taken up and got it for her. Afterward, she went back and took her time hand-washing the bloodstains out of her clothes in the guest bathroom. The curtain bar suspended atop the bathtub looked like it'd been stuck to the white-tiled walls with chewing gum, but it held when she hung her clothes on it to dry. Satisfied, Zoey headed out of the house.

. . .

Sunshine warmed Zoey's face as she walked the few blocks from Poppy's house to the boardwalk. The pressure in both her belly and her shoulders eased, and she began to feel a little proud. As scary as it had seemed, she'd survived getting her first period. She was officially a woman, like Mami and the girls at school. It made her feel closer to Mami even, knowing that they had shared the same experience. But Zoey's thoughts quickly returned to the men in her family. She'd been able to keep Dad and José from arguing back at the house, but how much longer before they went at it again? She understood why José often got upset with Dad. Sometimes she wished they could pick one place and stay there, too. But Dad also did the best he could, especially without Mami there anymore to help. He needed his kids to support his dreams so that, in turn, he'd feel well enough to take care of them. *Why doesn't José get it?* she wondered glumly.

She cheered up as she neared Poppy's bowling alley. The ocean stretched beautifully beside her, blue and sparkly, dotted with swimmers and boogie boards. Finally, the big red sign that said GONZO'S BOWLING ALLEY on one corner AND FUN on the other loomed ahead, a comfortingly familiar sight. Her family had spent two weeks with Poppy every summer before Mami's heart attack, and she loved visiting Gonzo's. She'd noticed the place seemed a bit smaller and less overwhelming when they'd come back last year for Abuela's funeral. But that had been a quick trip, and Zoey herself had grown since then. She was tall enough to reach the A on "alley" now. Trying to grab it had always been a game with José, one Zoey always lost. She grinned and gave the A a pat. It came loose in her hand, nearly smacking Zoey in the head. *Uh oh.* She stood there for a moment, debating what to do. She knew she should tell Poppy, but what if she got in trouble? In a split-second decision, Zoey left the A swinging upside down, hoping no one had seen. Maybe she could sneak back with one of the hammers from Poppy's basement later and try to fix it.

Inside, Poppy stood behind the shoe rental counter, frowning at his ancient laptop. When he spotted Zoey, he closed the computer and grinned.

"Hey, Poppy, *cómo*, um, how you doing?" Zoey said, struggling to remember the Spanish words her mom had used when Zoey was a little girl to ask Poppy how business was going.

Poppy shook his head, and pointed the blue pen he always kept in his pocket at Zoey.

"Did you forget all your Spanish, *mija*?" he asked, his voice playfully accusing.

"No," Zoey said, not wanting to disappoint.

Poppy raised his eyebrows and said a bunch of stuff in Spanish that Zoey didn't understand.

"I change my answer to *sí*," Zoey said, her lips curving up sheepishly, and Poppy laughed.

"It's okay, I teach you again this summer, eh?"

"*Sí*," Zoey agreed.

"Tell me that's not the only word you remember." Poppy groaned.

"I'm sure more will come back to me soon. So how's business going?" Zoey asked. School had just ended, and she wasn't in the mood to be quizzed on her Spanish skills.

"Okay. A little slow today, *mija*," Poppy said, waving a hand at the window. "Such a pretty day. No one wants to be inside bowling or playing games. Everybody is at the beach swimming. We do better when it rains."

Zoey glanced around. One skinny guy in a rock band tee rolled a spare. Beside him, a girl with massive French-manicured nails held up a tie-dyed ball and made duck lips at her phone, snapping a selfie. A couple of lanes away, an elderly couple in matching orthopedic sneakers took careful turns and bickered over where to go next for lunch. The rest of the arcade was empty, save for a thirty-something woman chasing her rowdy toddler around the broken air hockey table. Yellow caution tape cordoned off most of the game machines, even Skee-Ball, Zoey's favorite.

"Alex, don't you want to play a game?" the lady asked the little boy, finally catching his hand.

"Noooooo! They no work! I want Mommy's phone! PLAY GAME ON MOMMY'S PHONE!" he demanded, trying to rip open his mother's purse.

The mom sighed. She swooped the toddler into her arms, where he began to scream variations of "Want to play game on Mommy's phone!"

So cute, but so loud, Zoey thought to herself.

"I'm sorry. My son is only three. We're, ah, going through a little tantrum phase, and I think he needs a nap," the mom apologized to no one in particular, rushing out the door.

Poppy smiled and called "No worries" after them.

"You know, I remember when you were like that," he said to Zoey, coming around the counter to sit down in the folding chair beside the out-of-service Pac-Man.

"*Me?*" Zoey was appalled.

"*Ay ay ay, los gritos* when Abuela and I took you to the beach and tried to teach you to swim!" Poppy shook his head fondly. "You told us you were scared of sharks. We tell you, 'There's no sharks, *mija.*' You don't believe us. My little *jefa.* You want to tell us what to do. You order us to leave the beach and take you to Disney World instead. You screamed so loud I think my old neighbors hear you back in *la Habana vieja*."

Poppy laughed at the memory. Zoey felt her cheeks redden, especially at hearing her childhood nickname, *jefa*, again, which means "boss." She didn't feel like that title fit her. To be a boss, you have to be loud and confident. That certainly wasn't who she was anymore—in fact, she doubted whether she had ever been that assertive.

"Your brother was the opposite. José go running into the water, *sin los salvavidas*, the second his feet touch the sand. I remember your mami diving in to save him, even though she hate the water more than you. When she was a kid, all her friends would go to the beach. And she'd go and bring books to read. No one could get even her pinky toe *en el agua*."

Poppy's gaze was far away beneath his glasses. Zoey smiled, but thinking of her mom made her both happy and sad. She headed to the bin with the returned shoes, avoiding eye contact.

"Can I do anything to help? Maybe tidy those for you?" She didn't wait for Poppy to respond, and picked up a basket full of rental shoes to sort by size.

"Sure, *gracias, mija*," Poppy said, giving himself a

little shake and standing up to frown at the accounting software on his computer once more.

"By the way, the A in 'alley' is falling off the sign outside," Zoey said. She held her breath, waiting to see if Poppy would ask her how it got loose. She didn't know whether she was relieved or worried when he didn't.

"I'll fix it eventually," Poppy said, but his tone didn't match his words. He sounded depressed and glanced around at all the broken machines in the arcade as if they were ganging up on him. Remembering that Dad had warned José not to ask Poppy for money, Zoey wondered if maybe her grandpa couldn't afford to fix his sign and mentally kicked herself for breaking it.

To make up for the sign, Zoey shined the rental shoes until they gleamed. She'd been working for at least an hour when Poppy's next customer walked into Gonzo's. But the middle-aged man wiping his sweaty forehead with the sleeve of what looked like an expensive designer suit didn't much look like he wanted to bowl. Poppy glanced up when he heard the bell on the door chime. And when he saw who it was, Zoey noticed her grandfather stood up straighter—the same way Dad did when he wanted to assert his authority over José. Had Dad learned that habit from Poppy?

"Mr. Silos," Poppy addressed the man. "How are you?"

"Wishing it was December. It sure is a hot one out there," the man replied, gesturing toward the boardwalk outside.

Poppy nodded, but said nothing. No small talk about the weather? Obviously this was no ordinary customer. Wondering what was up, Zoey grabbed a broom and began sweeping the floor closer to where the guy in the suit was standing, so she could eavesdrop better. Poppy continued staring politely at the man, his back still stiff.

"Mr. Gonzalez, I'm here because I hope you've reconsidered my offer. It's more than fair."

Poppy's face turned pinker than the Barbie convertible he'd given Zoey when she was four. "I already told you, Mr. Silos. My answer is absolutely not."

"But—"

"No," Poppy said, his voice quiet but firm. "I will not sell to your company."

"Be reasonable, Mr. Gonzalez. We're offering you a decent profit margin, and you're facing eviction otherwise. The clock is ticking." Mr. Silos tapped his fat, gold, diamond-studded watch. "The deal I'm offering here is a win-win. This is a no-brainer."

Poppy sucked in his breath, and Zoey could tell he was trying very hard not to yell at Mr. Silos. Finally, Poppy spoke in a tone even lower and sterner than before.

"My answer remains no. *Buen día*, Mr. Silos. I hope you have a nice day."

Mr. Silos gawked at Poppy as if he'd sprouted a unicorn horn and shimmering blue mane, but finally appeared to get the message. He shook his wrist with the fancy watch in the air, mouthed "the clock is ticking" once more, and left.

Poppy exhaled as the glass door chimed shut and leaned over the counter, rubbing the gray hair above his temples.

"What was that all about?" Zoey asked.

Poppy jumped as if he'd forgotten Zoey was there.

"*Ay, mija*, it's nothing for you to worry about." Poppy waved a hand dismissively through the air, like Mr. Silos was nothing more than a fruit fly to be shooed away from the bananas. But Zoey didn't buy his casual act for a second. Dad was right. Poppy was in big trouble.

"It sounds like there's a lot to worry about!"

Poppy tsked, waving another dismissive hand. "*Mira*, every business has its headaches. My headache is named Mr. Silos. Yes, it's been a little slow at the bowling alley. Yes, if it doesn't turn around soon, then I have to close in a few weeks—"

A few weeks?! Zoey gasped.

"But I'm going to turn it around, Zoey. I don't want

you to worry, eh?" Poppy glanced down at her and smiled.

"Mr. Silos said you were going to get evicted though." Zoey's eyes widened into dinner plates.

"Mr. Silos just works for a big development company that wants to tear down the bowling alley and make a fancy new hotel for tourists. So, *mija*, he comes here to talk about the worst-case scenario and try to scare me. But no, your Poppy is no coward, eh?" He shook a finger in the air. "Absolutely not. This place, it's been in our family too many decades. I raise your mami here. I won't sell. I can't," Poppy said earnestly. His cloudy brown eyes looked far away again.

Zoey wondered what her grandfather was remembering. Her own bowling alley memories were all like abridged YouTube ads. A collage of snippets, each lasting only a few seconds. Mami laughing when five-year-old Zoey rolled the bowling ball from between her legs and it got stuck halfway down the lane, followed by Mami chasing after her when Zoey went down the lane to roll the ball the rest of the way. Dad shooting mini basketball hoops with José, while Mami and Zoey cheered them on, waiting for their turn. Mami showing Zoey how to shine rental shoes behind the counter. Abuela and Poppy handing Mami free lollipops from the prize basket that cost customers ten tickets apiece, for Zoey and José's dessert that night.

Zoey glanced back up at Poppy. He looked so forlorn
that her heart ached at the sight. Forget the broken sign.
Poppy had bigger problems to worry about. But right
then, Zoey's heartache solidified into steely resolve. She
was going to figure out a way to save the bowling alley,
no matter what.

3

Back at the house, Zoey tried talking to Poppy
about Mr. Silos's visit, but Poppy wasn't cooperating.

"Poppy, I want to talk about Mr. S—"

"*¿Qué?*" Poppy said, burying his head in the refrigerator to find the ingredients for tonight's dinner. "Sorry,
mija. I can't hear you. I look for the onions now!"

Zoey waited beside the fridge until Poppy finally
shut the door.

"I was saying—"

Poppy jumped, nearly dropping his onions on the
floor.

"*Ay, mija*, so sorry. I can't hear you over the music.
We talk later." Poppy shrugged helplessly, but Zoey had
just seen him poke at the volume button on the ancient
radio/cassette player on his counter. Indeed, the voice of

Julio Iglesias suddenly rocketed ten times louder out of Abuela's old tape. Frustrated, Zoey gave up trying to talk to Poppy and vowed to try again to get his attention later that night, maybe over dinner.

The result of Poppy's insistent culinary avoidance was *ropa vieja*, a traditional Cuban dish that translated in English to "old clothes." Ugh. Zoey had zero desire to taste it. Sure, the stuff looked innocently enough like shredded beef, but it probably tasted like old socks. Otherwise, what was up with the name? She pushed the meat to one side and dug into her yellow rice with peas instead.

"*Ropa vieja* was your mami's favorite food when she was your age," Poppy said in his thick accent, smiling sadly. The skin around his glasses crinkled like tissue paper.

José served himself seconds and paused at the kitchen counter, practically inhaling his beef before heading back for thirds. "Man, we haven't eaten like this in so long," he said. The way he eyed the slow cooker reminded Zoey of Pooh Bear beaming at a long-lost pot of honey.

"*Come más. Come más,*" Poppy urged them all to eat more, shooting a Look at Dad that asked without saying out loud, *Why doesn't el Americano feed my grandchildren better?*

Dad pretended not to see the Look. "Big news, guys!" he said instead. He tossed his napkin on the table and leaned forward eagerly.

Zoey's stomach churned, even though she'd just bitten into her *ropa vieja* and found the tender beef's peppery seasoning delightful. Usually, whenever Dad announced "big news," what he *meant* was "time for a big move."

Big news: We're leaving Boston to fulfill my lifelong goal of starting up my own bar and grill in Las Vegas!

Big news: My cousin in Colorado needs an assistant manager at his sporting goods store. Goodbye, Nevada deserts! Hello, skis and snowboards!

Big news: New family business in Silicon Valley! We're off to repurpose dead cell phones into inspirational fridge magnets!

But Zoey didn't want to move again. Twelve states in twelve years was more than enough. Plus, they'd only gotten to Poppy's house three days ago! Zoey had just finished unpacking, and for the first time since Mami died, Zoey felt close to her mother again. She *really* didn't want to let that feeling go. José crossed his arms and leaned back in his chair beside Zoey, shaking his head and looking like a younger, angry version of their dad.

"I have this buddy, Ryan Antoli. From high school. He's done real good the past few years, owns a motorcycle dealership. He needs a new salesperson," Dad said, pouring himself a tall glass of soda. "And you're looking at him!"

"Where's the dealership?" José asked, sucking in his cheeks.

"Ah, that's the best part," Dad said. "Your old man's got a job lined up in the Big Apple!"

Zoey sighed, and immediately felt bad for not mustering up more enthusiasm. Dad looked super excited about his new gig. Maybe this dream would actually stick.

"Where'd the cardboard boxes go?" All her packing things had disappeared from the front hallway yesterday. She'd figured Dad had thrown them out because they were planning to stay awhile. But they would need them now to repack.

"You don't need to pack, *mija*," Poppy told Zoey, patting her arm. "You're staying home."

Zoey's heart floated up to the ceiling at the word. She was home? Home. Home! That meant Zoey could look forward to school in the fall without dread. They'd be at the Jersey Shore with Poppy long enough for her to try out for extracurricular activities. Maybe she'd make a junior varsity sports team. Or join the debate club, like Mami.

"So you'll be commuting?" Zoey turned to Dad. "Are you taking the train or driving? Are you going to get back really late every night? If I make the girls' soccer team, do you think you'll be able to get back in time for my games?"

Dad frowned. "Kiddo, you're talking at least a four-hour round trip with traffic. It's too far to commute every day."

Confused, Zoey's eyes darted between Dad and Poppy. "I don't understand. Are we moving or not?"

"*I'm* going to New York City. I'll crash on Ryan's couch while I get settled," Dad said matter-of-factly.

Dad's words completely knocked the wind out of her, like the time she and José had gone water tubing in Delaware and she'd been flung off, smacking hard into waves made in the boat's wake.

Now suddenly Zoey felt like she was back in the water again, out of control and watching Dad speed off to a new adventure alone. But maybe she was overreacting, Zoey thought, trying to calm herself. Surely Dad didn't mean he was really leaving them. He just needed a day or two to find their new apartment, Zoey reassured herself, and started breathing again.

But beside her, José's mouth thinned into a grim line.

"You're leaving." There was no question in José's tone, just accusation.

"It's only temporary," Dad said, avoiding eye contact and scrolling through his phone.

Zoey stared at Dad, silently willing him to look up. Despite all of his harebrained schemes, this was the first time he had ever talked about living without them. No, without *her*, Zoey realized with a jolt. Dad was only leaving *her*, since José would be at college soon.

"How long?" Zoey asked, her voice small. Moving suddenly sounded better than being abandoned by the only parent she had left. But Zoey was afraid if she said that out loud, then José would get all protective and shout at Dad. The last thing any of them needed was another huge fight.

"I don't know, kiddo. I have the job on a trial basis. When the probation period's up, I'll come to get you."

He turned his wide blue eyes on Zoey then, and she knew what he needed her to say. That she'd be okay. That everything was great. "Peacemaker" was Zoey's role in the family, the same way José's was "realist." Whenever José yanked Dad down to reality, Zoey dusted Dad off and launched him back toward the stars. Mami used to do both, could balance Dad out with a single loving phrase, but ever since she'd died, the Finolio siblings split the job between them. If Mami were here, she would've asked Dad to join her in the kitchen, then convinced him in soft whispers not to leave while they cut up flan for dessert.

Zoey glanced away, frantically trying to think of a way to make Dad stay. For the first time ever, she didn't want to just tell Dad that she was okay with his "big news." Her gaze landed on a gold-framed photo of Mami on the boardwalk with Poppy and Abuela, in front of the bright red sign for Gonzo's. Every letter was lit by a necklace of tiny yellow lights. Suddenly Zoey had an idea of how she might convince Dad not to go.

"Wait, hang on, Dad. You can't leave because we have to save the bowling alley—"

"Zoey!" Poppy interrupted sharply.

Zoey hesitated, but only for a moment. "There's this mean guy who wants to evict Poppy and turn his bowling alley into a hotel! But I've been thinking, and maybe we can save the bowling alley if we fix it up. You could stay and help with the repairs. We'll get new customers and make enough to pay off the mortgage and—"

"Zoey! That's enough. I told you I don't want you worrying about grown-up problems. That's what the adults are for," Poppy said, shooting some major side-eye at Dad.

"The bowling alley is my concern, and *only* my concern."

Dad nodded, exhaling loudly. "Listen to your Poppy, Zoey. He knows what he's doing. Just like I know what I'm doing. We're all working through something here. I have a good feeling about selling motorcycles—I just can't afford to move us all to Manhattan yet. And lots of kids spend the summer with their grandparents. This is just temporary," he said again, giving Zoey's hand a quick squeeze. "I should have enough for my own place in the city by the time José goes to college, and then you can come bunk with your old man. Sound good?"

No, Zoey thought, gawking at her father. What sounded good to her was staying put together as a family. Mami had always said, *"Lo más importante del mundo es la familia."* The most important thing in the world is family. Had Dad somehow forgotten that?

"What happened to your dream of starting that food truck, Finolio's Famous Grilled Cheeses?" Zoey asked, desperately grasping for another reason to make him stay. "Isn't that why we moved here to begin with? Let's feed all those hungry people at the beach! You make the best mozzarella-muenster-provolone blend in the world!"

Dodging Zoey's gaze, Dad checked his phone again.

His free hand combed uncomfortably through his thick brown hair. Poppy crossed his arms at the same time as José and raised his eyebrows. "Michael, aren't you going to answer your daughter's question?"

Dad finally put his phone down on the table. "Look, I didn't realize how expensive buying a new truck would be. Or how many regulations applied. I'd basically need a full kitchen. And developing a whole menu around just one dish, especially a simple one like grilled cheese, turned out to be a lot harder than I thought."

I could help, Zoey thought excitedly, imagining tomatoes, caramelized onions, all the toppings they could add to create a whole line of famous grilled cheeses. Maybe even *ropa vieja* on rye. But before she had a chance to pipe up, Poppy interrupted.

"Excuses, excuses, excuses," he muttered in disgust. "*¡Ya basta!* I am so sick of your excuses, Michael! In the twenty years I know you, you never change! The only thing I can count on with you is that you will never— *nunca*—amount to *nada!*" Poppy banged his fist on the table, and Zoey jumped along with the water cups.

Dad's jaw twitched beneath the shadow of his beard. "I can't help it if things don't always go as planned."

But his choice of words only seemed to further infuriate Poppy, whose face turned purple. A vein popped out on his neck, zigzagging from his shirt collar all the way to his ear. "*Ya sé.*"

"I'm teaching them to follow their dreams," Dad said slowly, glaring at Poppy. Next to Zoey, José scoffed.

"No dreams, *tontería*! You have every privilege in the world and you waste it! You know how hard it is for my family coming to a new country to build our lives? No. You don't know. You were born here. You can do anything. But you don't. And you are no longer a young man with no one to support, Michael," Poppy said, his accent growing thicker in his exasperation. "You are a father of two who quits every single job he starts. And it's not like you even have *one*—" Poppy pointed his index finger at Dad's shirt "—big passion you try to make work. Oh no, you are not a painter or a poet or a chef like my Jasmeen! No, you have dream of the day, like my restaurant in the bowling alley used to have soup of the day. You're not special— you have specials!" Poppy shouted, waving his hands for emphasis. "Today grilled cheese, tomorrow motor-cycles. But *qué va, mijo*, you are forty-four years old! Time to grow up."

"Not that it's any of your business, but Jasmeen and I had an equal marriage. I supported her dreams," Dad said, spitting out the words like they were marbles that had been stuck in his throat for five years. "And she supported mine."

"My daughter did everything," Poppy said, his voice rising. "She raised the kids, kept house, and used her salary to bail you out of every mess you make. Equal marriage? You take all the dreams and leave her all the stress. That was equal? You work her to death! *¡Pobrecita!* No wonder my baby had the heart attack at only thirty-nine."

At this revelation, Zoey's own heart nearly stopped. Mami's death wasn't Dad's fault. It . . . it couldn't be. Right? She glanced at José to see what he thought, but her brother looked as shocked as she felt. His eyes were wide, staring at Poppy.

"I won't have you speak about me that way in front of my own children, Rafael," Dad said, his voice low and deadly. His eyes narrowed into thin slits.

Poppy crossed his arms again and an angry train of Spanish words barreled from his lips. The only word Zoey caught was her mom's name, Jasmeen.

But Dad stood up so fast his chair fell backward onto the brown linoleum floor with a loud bang. "How dare you!" Dad roared.

Zoey gaped at him, shocked by his sudden anger and surprised that he'd understood Poppy. She'd thought Dad, the only non-Cuban in their family, spoke even less

Spanish than she did. After all, it was he who'd hidden away all of Mami's Spanish music CDs when she died. Taken away every reminder of her culture—from the drawings of guardian angels beneath their mattresses to the hourglass-shaped *cafetera Cubana* she'd used to make strong coffee when Dad went on business trips. But apparently he understood plenty.

"This is my house, I can speak the truth as I see it!" Poppy shouted, getting to his feet now, fists balled at his sides. Both men leaned forward menacingly with only the wooden table between them.

Zoey's family had always been loud. *Really* loud. Though their arguments were never physical. But now for the first time in her life, Zoey was afraid that Dad and Poppy might actually exchange blows.

"Stop it! Please! Mami wouldn't want you to fight. Everyone *just stop!*"

Startled, Poppy and Dad glanced at Zoey as if they'd forgotten she and José were still listening. The invisible fishing line reeling them toward each other was suddenly, thankfully, broken. Dad took a step back. Blinking, Poppy began cleaning his glasses with a napkin.

"No more fighting," Zoey ordered again, choking back tears. And then she bolted up the stairs to her mother's old room.

. . .

"It's going to be okay," José told Zoey later. He was her third visitor that evening. Not long after their disaster of a dinner, Dad had shuffled in and sheepishly stroked her hair for a couple of minutes. Then he'd confirmed he was leaving early the next morning and asked her to text or call him every day. About an hour later, Poppy had checked in, mumbling about the importance of a good night's sleep before vanishing into the local news and his nightly cup of *manzanilla* tea. It was the closest either of them would come to apologizing for upsetting her.

"No. It won't," Zoey answered without glancing up at José, who'd perched on the edge of her bed. "Dad's moving without us, and Poppy's losing his bowling alley. Everything sucks."

Zoey couldn't imagine not having Dad or José around, but soon—very, very soon—she'd have to get used to life without both of them. Zoey curled under the soft ivory quilt her grandmother had made for Mami, wishing she was one of the tiny embroidered birds on it. Birds never had to worry about their families falling apart.

"We can handle the bowling alley," José said confidently. "I've been Googling all night. I'll fix the broken machines in the arcade. You'll help me. We'll get the place running better than it has in years."

Zoey grunted, her head still buried under Mami's blanket. The Advil had long since worn off and the cramps were starting again. When would this day end?

"Come on, come out of there," José said, yanking the quilt off her head. "Don't worry about Dad, either. You know he'll be back here in five minutes, chasing some new dream. Maybe this time with a motorcycle. That would be sweet, wouldn't it?"

"I guess so."

"And we'll be too busy helping Poppy to miss him."

"I guess."

"Aaaand," José said, dragging the word out for dramatic effect, "at least we know we get to stay in one place for the summer. This might be an amazing opportunity to, like, you know, make new friends or something."

"Or something," Zoey repeated.

"I don't know about you, but I get tired of hanging out with myself."

"I don't. I like hanging out with you," Zoey said, her lips involuntarily lifting into a tiny smile. José grinned back and scooped Zoey into a quick hug before padding off soundlessly in his socks.

"I mean it," Zoey called after José, feeling better.

"Good! Cause you'll be seeing plenty of me when we grease that pinball machine tomorrow. Gotta work fast to finish before college starts," he called back, making Zoey's stomach cramp up again. She wished José hadn't reminded her that he was leaving in a few weeks. That one way or another, the people she loved always left her behind.

The following morning was gray and rainy—it matched Zoey's mood perfectly. She'd pretended to be asleep when Dad slipped into her room to say goodbye at the crack of dawn, because she thought it would be too painful to say the words, then cried at the window as she watched him leave. Now Zoey was trapped in the bowling alley, passing screwdrivers and wrenches to José, and wishing she could go outside and kick all her blah gray feelings into a reassuringly black-and-white soccer ball.

"Hammer?" José lay under the broken pinball machine. All Zoey could see of him was his legs and his hand sticking out.

He'd been working for three hours, and Zoey was starting to wonder whether trying to fix the pinball machine was pointless. Not just because José wasn't a professional repairman and quite likely didn't know what he was doing, but because, according to Poppy, Gonzo's should've been busy on a rainy day like today. And it was totally empty. Apparently all the beachgoers had decided to stay home or go to the movies.

How would Zoey ever find Poppy more customers in time to save his bowling alley?

"Pliers?" José requested.

Zoey handed them over without glancing up from the picture of a soccer field she was doodling on a napkin. Even if the weather had been cooperating, Zoey didn't know if there were any soccer fields near Poppy's house. She might not be able to play soccer again until school started. Wherever *that* might be.

"I'm heading out to pick up *la pizza*," Poppy called. "*Mija*, take care of the customers if any come."

"Okay," Zoey called back, watching her grandfather through the window as he opened his old blue umbrella beneath the overhang outside the bowling alley's front door.

"He doesn't sound like he thinks customers are coming," she crouched down to whisper to José under the table.

"Why are you whispering? We're the only two people here."

"Exactly."

"Well, that's why we're trying to fix the place up, isn't it?"

"I know. It's just, I don't know, shouldn't Poppy care more? He doesn't sound worried. And before the fight with Dad, he kept changing the subject every time I tried to talk to him about the bowling alley."

"I think he just doesn't want *you* to worry," José said.

Ding! The bell on the door chimed. José stuck his head out from under the pinball machine and gently nudged Zoey's dirty white sneaker with his toe.

"Maybe things are looking up. Go mind the counter while I keep working on this." He disappeared beneath the machine again.

Sighing, Zoey got to her feet, then froze when she saw Fashion Girl—the one who'd helped her yesterday—chatting animatedly with another girl. There were also two boys with them. They leaned over the shoe rental counter, craning their necks to find an employee. Feeling her face flush, Zoey slid quickly behind the cash register.

"Hi, guys. Welcome to Gonzo's. How can I help you?" Zoey said, imitating the bright, professional voice she remembered Abuela always used with customers before she got too sick to help Poppy in the bowling alley a couple of summers ago.

The taller boy had wide brown eyes flecked with

hazel, dark skin, and a solemn expression that made him seem both cute and slightly mysterious. "We need to rent shoes and a bowling lane," he said, putting a wad of bills down on the counter. "I'll take a size nine."

Zoey nodded.

"I've never seen you in here before," the shorter boy said. He was pale, with straight brown hair that fell into his glasses and a round face that curved easily into a grin.

"This place belongs to my grandpa. I'm just visiting for the summer," Zoey explained.

She wondered as the words came out of her mouth whether they were true. Would Dad make good on his promise to let her move back in with him when he got settled in the city? Or would she live alone with Poppy forever while José was in college and Dad was off selling motorcycles or chasing some new dream?

"That's so cool! You're, like, the luckiest person ever to spend all your time in a fun place like this."

He looked around appreciatively, grinning at the sign for Skee-Ball. Zoey glanced around too, remembering when she used to think her mom was the luckiest for having been raised as the princess of her parents' arcade. Parties and prizes and games galore! Now though, she wondered how much time and effort had gone into keeping this place nice all those years. While Zoey got the shoes, she stole a glance at the girls, who were preoccupied with showing each other videos on their phones. They looked like they'd just stepped out of Forever 21 or H&M or some other fabulous website in their sparkly leggings and perfectly applied eye shadow and neon nail polish. Fashion Girl with the purple highlights wore a pink plaid shirt that somehow managed to look chic instead of like a tablecloth. Her snooty friend's long blond hair was tied in two perfect French braids. Bright beaded bracelets that matched her yellow and green nail polish encircled Snooty Friend's wrists. *They're like walking fields of daisies, bursting with color,* Zoey thought. Next to them, Zoey felt like a lima bean plant. Bland and boring.

She gave the boys their shoes. The girls stepped up to the counter next, and Zoey couldn't avoid eye contact with Fashion Girl any longer.

"Hey! It's you! How're you doing?" Fashion Girl grinned at Zoey.

"You guys know each other?" the other girl asked. Her tone sounded surprised. The way she looked Zoey up and down from head to toe made Zoey even more self-conscious about her frizzy ponytail and her faded superhero tee that she'd inherited from José.

"We just met when my mom took me shopping

for sunblock and stuff yesterday. Before we went to the beach," Fashion Girl told Snooty Friend, then winked at Zoey, as if to assure her she wasn't going to tell anyone about helping Zoey through her first period. Zoey's stomach unclenched a little. Maybe her secret was safe.

"Oh," Snooty Friend said, losing interest. She glanced at the shoe bins behind Zoey. "Size seven."

Zoey nodded and grabbed a pair.

"I'm Isabelle Levine, by the way, but you can call me Isa," Fashion Girl told Zoey when Zoey found her size. "And that's Lacey Johnston." Hearing her name, Snooty Friend half-smiled and half-waved from the bench where she laced up her shoes.

"That's Patrick Donoway. He's captain of our bowling team." Isa tilted her head toward the taller guy. "And last but not least, that's Tyler Tate." The boy with the round face offered Zoey a friendly wave.

"Oh, uh, nice to meet you guys. My name is Zoey Finolio." Zoey smiled shyly at the group and led them to the bowling lane that was the least scuffed.

Lacey immediately walked over to the automatic scorer for their lane and pushed the buttons. The screen over their heads stayed blank.

"Is this thing working? It wasn't last time we bowled."

"Sorry, I think that computer's still down. But all the

lanes are open. Here, let me just . . ." Zoey trailed off, pressing the button down hard on the scorer for the lane beside them, praying silently it would turn on. The screen above jumped to life, asking for the first player to enter his or her name.

"Here, this scorer connects you to lane seven," Zoey said. Patrick sat down to type in his name. Tyler began picking up the different bowling balls, testing their weight in his hands.

"We should go back to the alley with the black light and music," Lacey whispered loudly to Isa behind Zoey's back.

"That place was too crowded," Tyler groaned, settling on a sleek white ball with red swirls that reminded Zoey of an enormous baseball and practicing his bowling moves in the corner.

"And it was way too hard to see," Patrick said, standing up and stretching his legs. "I'm done typing. Who's next?"

Isa sat down to enter her name into the computer.

"Plus, it's cheap here, and no one from the competition can see our moves or try to steal them." Patrick picked up a fluorescent yellow ball and mimed rolling a strike. Lacey rolled her eyes and whipped out her phone from her pocket.

"Fine, but I'm sure we can find another place that's easier to practice in and isn't a dump." Lacey flipped one of her perfect French braids over her shoulder.

Zoey had heard enough.

"This place is *not* a dump. It's been here more than forty years—it's an *institution*. If you don't like it, there's the door," Zoey said, pointing. "Take your money back and get out!"

Hands on her hips, Zoey glared at Lacey. But, though she refused to show it, Zoey regretted the words the second they were out of her mouth. Poppy needed every paying customer, even the rude ones. How could she turn away good money? She should have just gritted her teeth and ignored Lacey. For her part, Lacey glanced up from her phone with an incredulous expression, like she thought Zoey was a space alien who'd just landed in front of her from Mars. Patrick stood up, panic written all over his face.

"Please don't kick us out. I'm sorry, and Lacey is sorry," he said.

Lacey opened her mouth as if to protest, but Patrick cut her off with a warning look.

"I'm captain of our bowling team, and I take responsibility for all my members. Lacey *is* sorry," he said pointedly, before Lacey could speak. He turned to glare at her again, and this time Lacey shut her mouth. "We want to stay and bowl, okay?"

"Okay," Zoey said quietly.

"Why don't you play with us?" Isa asked, smoothly inserting herself between Lacey and Zoey. "I bet you're really good!"

Zoey blushed. "Oh, uh, actually I—"

"Pizza's here!" Poppy called, sailing in the front door with two big boxes. He lit up when he saw Zoey and the group of kids. "I got plain cheese and veggie. You guys want some? ¡Ven y come! Plenty to go around."

"Awesome! I'm starving," Tyler said, returning his bowling ball to the rack and heading straight over to Poppy. "Thank you."

"Me too," Isa said. "Come on, Lace."

Lacey's lips flared in a duck pout, but she grudgingly followed Isa.

"Thanks, Poppy," Zoey said. "I'll go get some plates and napkins."

The little café at the far back of the arcade used to be a favorite spot for locals and a hidden gem for tourists. Zoey walked past the empty dining area, recalling a time when every table had been filled and some customers had to stand to eat. Inside the kitchen, Zoey flipped on a light. There were cobwebs everywhere and dust on the appliances. Zoey blinked back tears, imagining the kitchen as it had once been. Mami and Abuela working alongside each other, chopping and dicing and stirring, perfectly in sync. Abuela shouting out orders, to be heard above the radio. Even though Mami was the amazing trained chef in the outside world, Abuela's word was the only one that had mattered in here.

Abuela was the best, Zoey thought, remembering how easily and efficiently her grandmother dealt with people. Once, a cranky old guy slipped and fell in his bowling lane. He hadn't suffered more than a bruised butt, and it was his own fault for crossing the foul line, but he yelled insults and threats all the same. Until Abuela brought him ice, chatted with him for a little while, and gave him a hamburger on the house. They were laughing like old friends by the end of the night. And then there was the time Abuela hosted a reality TV crew and sweet-talked the producers into coming back to film the birthday party of a cast member's daughter in the arcade. After the show aired, Zoey remembered Mami saying the publicity had really put Gonzo's on the map. There was still a bulletin board pinned with photos of Zoey's grandparents and the reality TV stars hanging up near the front counter of the bowling alley.

Overcome by a rush of longing for her grandmother, Zoey wished she could ask Abuela about how to save Gonzo's. After all, she and Poppy had run it together for decades. Zoey took a deep breath to keep herself from crying, and went over to a supply closet near the back of the kitchen in search of paper goods. When she was younger, she'd been forbidden from actually setting foot in here, for fear that she might be burned or hurt by accident. But every so often Zoey had still stuck her head inside to watch and take a big whiff of the tantalizing smells coming from the pots on the stove. It felt strange now to be so near the oven; she kept waiting for Abuela to appear and chase her out with a spatula.

When Zoey returned, she saw Poppy had put the pizzas on an empty chair near their lane. She put the paper plates and napkins she'd found wrapped in plastic in the closet on the chair, and everyone dug in. Lacey made a show of daintily grabbing a slice and going off poker-faced to another lane to sit by herself. Sighing and casting an apologetic look at Zoey, Isa went to eat with her. In every school Zoey had attended, she knew that who you sat with at lunch mattered. She guessed Isa choosing to sit with Lacey now without making space on their bench for her meant Isa wasn't really her friend yet, which stung more than it should have, considering how they'd met. But then Patrick patted the chair across from him, and Zoey let herself relax as she sat down to eat beside Tyler. They intimidated her way less than Lacey and Isa. Talking to guys was so much easier for her than talking to other girls. It was just like talking to José. Plus, you didn't usually have to worry that guys would judge what you were wearing. Unless maybe you had a crush on one. But Zoey had far too much on her mind to fuss with crushes at the moment.

"Do you bowl, like, every day?" Patrick asked Zoey. He sounded, Zoey thought, a little envious.

Zoey shook her head. "We just moved to New Jersey from Florida. I mean, I bowled here and there with my brother when we visited Poppy in the summers. But I've never been on a team or anything."

Tyler shrugged. "We're all on our school team. Now we're preparing for the Summer Big Bowl Championship."

"And now that we don't have homework, we gotta try and practice as much as we can. I'm going to make sure this team maximizes its potential!" Patrick added. His feet tapped restlessly on the floor. He scarfed down his second slice like he couldn't wait to get started.

Tyler rolled his eyes, but laughed good-naturedly. "You're so intense, dude."

"I have to be intense to win," Patrick said, all business.

Tyler shook his head, looking equal parts amused and perplexed, and turned back to Zoey.

"Do you play sports? Were you on any teams in Florida?"

"Yeah, um, soccer," Zoey replied without elaborating. Dad had moved them from Miami last September, to Coral Springs last January, and to Homestead in April. Changing schools so many times hadn't really given her a chance to officially try out for a soccer team. But she still kicked the soccer ball around whenever—and wherever—she could.

"All right, time to play," Patrick announced.

"If you're not busy, you really should play with us," Isa called from the bench where she sat chatting with Lacey, renewing her offer from earlier. Isa smiled warmly. Lacey picked at her magenta nail polish, but didn't say anything.

Zoey's heart felt lighter—perhaps she and Isa might still become friends. But she hesitated. She wasn't very good at actual bowling. And she still hadn't figured out a way to help Poppy save the bowling alley. But Poppy had come over to start clearing away the empty boxes and he'd clearly overheard Isa.

"Go play with your new friends, *mija*," he said. "I don't need your help at the counter right now."

"Uh, yeah. Okay, sure," Zoey said finally. She smiled tentatively back at Isa, avoided eye contact with Lacey, and wondered if she was about to make a really big fool of herself.

Indeed, on her first try, Zoey rolled a gutter ball. Lacey went next and knocked down only one pin. She scowled at Zoey as if it were her fault. Zoey chewed the inside of her cheek and ignored her, reminding herself once more that Lacey was a paying customer and Poppy needed as many of those as possible. Isa rolled a perfect strike, which made Patrick super happy. Tyler seemed pleased enough with his spare, and decided to take Zoey under his wing.

"Step forward with the foot on the opposite side of the hand that's holding the ball, and slide the other leg behind you," he suggested, and to Zoey's surprise, Tyler's tip worked. She knocked down a couple of pins on her next turn.

Time slipped away. When Zoey next glanced up from the scoreboard, they were already on their second game, and Gonzo's buzzed with the chatter and thunderous strikes of several new lanes worth of bowlers. She saw José was still hanging out by the pinball machine. Only now instead of trying to fix it, he leaned over it, arms and face covered in grease, chatting with a girl around his age who didn't seem to mind his messy appearance all. Zoey approved of the girl's outfit—

dark blue capris over pink ballerina flats and a flowy, pink, pin-striped blouse with butterfly sleeves. The girl pulled her long, curly hair into a ponytail, laughing at something José said. Zoey giggled as José ran a hand through his own hair and jumped, probably realizing he looked like he'd stuck his head inside a bottle of olive oil. Watching her nerdy brother try to flirt always amused Zoey. But today she was having too much fun bowling to go tease him.

After five more games, Zoey's arms were sore and she needed a break. The others were sore too. And out of cash.

"That was my last five-dollar bill," Tyler said, rubbing his elbows and yawning. "And I'm sleepy."

"Yeah, I think we did enough for one day," chimed in Lacey, already scrolling through her texts.

"Our next practice is Thursday," Patrick said, checking the calendar on his phone. "Let's come back here to Gonzo's."

Lacey rolled her eyes at the beige paint peeling off the ceiling, but everyone else agreed.

"Could we order pizza again?" Isa asked Zoey. "I'll pay for mine next time."

"I'll go anywhere there's pizza," Tyler said, opening the last empty box and scavenging for crumbs.

His comment made a light bulb go off in Zoey's head. An idea for saving Poppy's bowling alley! Gonzo's didn't sell food anymore—just lollipops and candy in exchange for tickets from the prize display. But maybe all Poppy had to do to turn things around was offer a menu again. The bowling alley had thrived when Abuela was alive and Gonzo's offered lunch, dinner, and snacks. And Zoey couldn't remember the exact Spanish phrase, but Mami always used to say something to the effect of a happy stomach meant a happy heart. Maybe all they had to do was feed customers, and they'd show up in gaggles.

"We can definitely get pizza," Zoey promised, feeling hopeful.

After Isa and her friends left, Zoey pushed past the swinging pink door into the kitchen again, determined now to figure out how to offer a full menu again for Poppy to serve customers. The kitchen, however, had other ideas. Having gotten used to sleeping all day and all night, it refused to wake up and cooperate now. The industrial-size sink's pipes groaned like hibernating bears, declining to pour water when Zoey tried turning on the faucets. None of the burners on the professional stove worked either. Ditto for the oven and microwave. Inside the cabinets were filled with dust, and upon closer inspection, most of the pots and the pans were rusted and sticky—like maybe they hadn't been washed thoroughly enough after their last use. The bottom of Zoey's sneakers stuck to the celery-green tiled floor in some places, too.

But Zoey refused to be deterred. As Poppy had so tastily proved by cooking *ropa vieja* last night, the kitchen back at the house worked just fine.

5

Zoey soon discovered cooking at Poppy's house had its challenges too. Her grandparents had never believed in throwing away money on plastic ware—instead saving things like coffee cans and refilling them with other staples, so that almost no container in Poppy's pantry actually held the food on its label. Finding ingredients became a treasure hunt of sorts. Zoey unearthed flour in a tin meant for vanilla cookies, sugar in the peanut butter jar, and, to her great surprise, mini chocolate bars on the cusp of expiring inside a can of asparagus.

"Your Abuela used to worry about my sweet tooth," Poppy explained sadly when Zoey asked about that one. "So she hide the goodies in the healthy food. She used to say if I actually went looking for vegetables, then maybe I deserved a treat." He laughed fondly at the memory.

"One time, I opened the freezer and won the lottery. *Imagínate*, a whole pint of mint chocolate chip! Inside the broccoli."

Zoey giggled.

"*Ay*, that was a good day," he said, patting her shoulder and leaving Zoey to search for online recipes to try.

At first, Zoey didn't share her plan to relaunch the restaurant inside Gonzo's with her family, letting Poppy assume she'd just taken up a new hobby. But when Zoey spent the next two days baking as if she planned to feed the entire population of New Jersey, and possibly Connecticut, Poppy finally asked her what was up.

"You invite Willy Wonka over for dinner tonight without telling me, *mija*?" he joked, eyeing the bag bursting with chocolate chips that Zoey plopped on his kitchen island. "And you get, what? Every different kind? White chocolate. Dark chocolate. Milk chocolate. Even peanut butter?"

"Yup," Zoey said excitedly.

"José go with you? How you afford all this?"

"Oh, I had some birthday money saved up," she said airily. She'd already put away most of the groceries by the time Poppy walked in, and she didn't want him to know she'd spent a hundred and ten dollars, her entire life savings, buying more ingredients.

Poppy opened the oven. Zoey had stuffed four trays worth of puff pastries inside. Some filled with spinach and cheese. Others with potatoes and spices. Zoey inhaled, pleased with the scent that escaped the full oven. Her mouth watered.

"Who going to eat all this?" Poppy asked.

"I thought maybe we could reopen the café inside Gonzo's," Zoey said casually, hoping now that the food was already made (and delicious!), Poppy would say yes and finally let her help. She brushed past Poppy to stick a fork inside one of her creations. The mushroom and olive blend Zoey had thrown together tasted divine, if she did say so herself. She closed her eyes to savor the flavor, then grabbed another fork and offered Poppy a bite. "Maybe you'll get more customers if you sell food again."

"*Ay no, mija*, I thought I tell you I don't want you to worry," Poppy said, tsking. He tasted the bite Zoey offered him and closed his eyes too. "Very good. You a good chef like your mami. But you don't have to do all this for me."

"But I want to!" Zoey said. "And this reminds me of when I used to cook with Mami. We made *tres leches* cake and rice pudding with Abuela the last . . . a while back," Zoey said, stumbling over her words.

She'd been about to say *the last summer we were all*

together, but she didn't want to risk making Poppy sad. The memory was a happy one for her, though. Abuela had let her lick all the mixing bowls and spoons over Mami's halfhearted objection about ruining dinner. Her mother and grandmother had playfully bickered over what music to play on the ancient stereo. It was Mother's Day weekend, and Mami had bought the three of them hot pink, personalized aprons that said SWEET AND SASSY underneath pictures of giant winking pastries. Zoey's apron had sported a cupcake. Now, alternating between Abuela's Julio Iglesias cassettes and Mami's Whitney Houston CDs, Zoey felt them with her as she baked.

Poppy was unusually silent, staring at the wall.

"Why'd you stop selling food in the bowling alley?" Zoey asked, hoping to distract him from his thoughts. He didn't answer, turning to taste the fresh strawberry sauce simmering on the stove instead.

"Poppy, did you hear me? Why'd the café in Gonzo's close down permanently? Nothing in the kitchen there even works anymore."

Poppy's back stiffened.

"Your abuela got sick," he said quietly, avoiding Zoey's gaze. He busied himself cutting fresh strawberries and throwing them in a small ceramic bowl covered with yellow flowers that Zoey remembered buying at the dollar store with Abuela when she was six. Zoey held her breath, waiting for him to continue.

"Your grandma was the one in charge of the food. She do the cooking. When she get sick, it too hard for me to take care of her and the bowling alley and keep the café going *también*, so I just let it go," he said in a low voice, scooping vanilla ice cream into the bowl with the strawberries and drizzling Zoey's sauce on top. Zoey looked down at her shoes, worried that she'd gone too far with her questions.

"This sauce is amazing," he told her after a moment of awkward silence.

"Thanks," Zoey said, feeling her ears turn pink. She looked up to see Poppy smiling kindly at her. It gave her the courage to press on.

"Maybe now that I'm here we can open it again. I'll help you."

"*Echhhh.*" Poppy made a sound like he was simultaneously dismissing Zoey's idea and clearing his sinuses. "Our menu *está* outdated. I'd have to do something completely new *y no vale la pena*," he grumbled. "Nobody want just a simple home-cooked meal anymore. Now *todo es* fusion this and keto that and avocado on top with ten different kinds of mayonnaise."

"It could bring more customers in though."

He shook his head. "It no make a difference. People want to bowl, or they don't," he said stubbornly.

"But maybe—"

"I said no," Poppy said firmly. "You want to cook here, okay. But I don't want you to try to sell all this food inside the bowling alley. Understood?"

Zoey sighed and nodded. When Poppy left the kitchen, Zoey turned back to her sauce. She took out a spoon and tasted it for herself. It *was* good. Maybe she'd be as good a cook as Mami one day. Zoey squared her shoulders and started washing some of the dishes. If Poppy could be stubborn, then so could she. Technically, Poppy had banned her from selling food inside.

He hadn't said anything about *outside.*

The next day Zoey set up shop on the boardwalk right in front of Gonzo's about an hour after Poppy went in to work. Zoey was ready to fight Poppy on this; after all, she was holding the bake sale to help *him.* But when Poppy spotted her when he came out for a break, he only threw his hands up in exasperation and grabbed a brownie drizzled in fresh strawberry sauce. He didn't force her to move. He even smiled after tasting her strawberry sauce again, so Zoey exhaled and got down to business.

At first, everyone who walked by stopped to read Zoey's glittery blue BAKE SALE poster and snap up a sweet treat. But somehow after six hours, Zoey had barely made forty dollars. And she'd forgotten the bowling alley didn't have a working fridge. So Zoey's baked goods were on the verge of spoiling after just a couple of hours. Zoey also now realized the prices were too low. She should have charged at least two dollars a brownie, not fifty cents. She was going to lose all the money she'd put into Operation Save Gonzo's.

Zoey felt dumb, and wondered if this was how Dad felt too when his dream bubbles popped. Perhaps this was another reason why he was always so quick to move on to new ones. Thinking about Dad made Zoey miss him. She took out her phone and sent him a message.

Learned to bake this week. José likes my PB cookies, & Poppy likes my fudge chip brownies drizzled in strawberry sauce. Come visit soon. I'll make you both! ☺

She stared at her phone for a few minutes, but Dad didn't text back right away. Oh well. Maybe he was busy selling motorcycles. Maybe this dream would actually work out for him this time.

"Hey, Zoey!"

Zoey glanced up to find Isa fishing through a giant striped beach bag for exact change. She dropped two quarters in Zoey's jar and plucked a red velvet cupcake from her tray.

"Yummm," Isa said through a mouthful of crumbs. "Are you going to start selling these every day?"

"No," Zoey said, sighing. "Business has been kind of slow for Poppy lately. I was just trying to get more customers by selling food outside the bowling alley. But it's not really working. I think I'm done."

Isa looked pensive as she inhaled her cupcake and bought a second.

"It's a good idea though—selling food. Maybe you'd get more people if you offer the food inside."

"But Poppy didn't want me to sell my baked goods, and he definitely isn't going to cook food by himself," Zoey said glumly.

Isa pursed her lips, thinking out loud.

"There's this awesome sandwich shop a couple of blocks north on the boardwalk," she said, pointing. "The family who runs it are super nice—this girl Toni-Ann and her parents. She used to be my babysitter when I was a kid. They make the best avocado chicken in the world. I don't know what's in their seasoning, but I've never tasted anything like it. And the dipping sauces and the crispy fries, honestly, the whole menu's amazing. I bet more people would definitely want to go bowling if they thought they could grab a super yummy lunch at the same time, like multitask. Maybe Toni-Ann's family could partner with your grandpa to sell food inside the bowling alley?"

"Maybe," Zoey said, feeling a little more hopeful. Maybe Poppy would be open to selling food inside Gonzo's if he didn't have to cook it.

Isa grinned. "Think about it."

Suddenly, footsteps hammered on the boardwalk behind them.

"Isabelle!" Lacey ran up behind Isa and yanked her beach bag off her shoulder. "This. Is. So. Cute. Where'd you get it?"

"Outlet mall," Isa said, giving Lacey a hug hello and grabbing her bag back. She gasped. "I love your sandals."

"Thanks." Lacey preened, sticking out a foot so the green rhinestones on her flip-flops would twinkle in the sunlight. "They're new."

"Love!" Isa gushed again.

Lacey grinned, stretching her arms above her head. "Come on! What are you doing? Let's go to the beach!"

Isa lit up. "Sure! Want to come, Zoey?"

Zoey glanced down at the remains of her bake sale.

The morning rush had been busy, but the afternoon crowd didn't seem to want brownies that had been sitting in the heat for hours. Isa had been her only customer in the past hour.

"Sounds great," Zoey said. "Let me just run home to get changed."

Forty-five minutes later, slathered in SPF 30 and wearing a plain tank top with black capris, Zoey perched on a polka-dot beach towel beside Isa and Lacey. She still felt awkward about her lack of style in front of the other girls in their trendy two-pieces and sundresses. But her self-consciousness was starting to fade a little now. Mostly, she just felt uncomfortable because she still had her period and didn't feel like learning how to use a tampon so she could wear a bathing suit. Besides, her bathing suit probably didn't fit anymore. She hadn't gone swimming in over a year. And sure the ocean looked all fun and friendly, but Zoey was still afraid of the dangers you couldn't see from the shore: sharks, jellyfish, flesh-eating bacteria. She shivered despite the heat just thinking about it, and took a deep breath to clear her head. At least she'd met some kids to hang out with. Isa seemed genuinely nice. And Lacey might be a snob, Zoey thought, but at least she hadn't looked Zoey's outfit up and down today or crinkled her nose like Zoey's wardrobe wasn't up to her standards.

The Devil's Arithmetic was on their summer required reading list, so Isa and Lacey had both brought a copy. Lacey squinted behind giant sunglasses and cradled her phone close to reduce the sun's glare on her Kindle app. Zoey had brought a yellowed paperback copy of *A Wrinkle in Time* that she'd found on the childhood bookshelf in Mami's old room. But sweating under the bright sun, Zoey couldn't concentrate on the words in front of her. José was usually the one who reminded Dad to enroll her in a new school. But soon he wouldn't be here to do that anymore. And she didn't even know whether she'd go to the same middle school as Isa and Lacey, or if Dad would swoop in and really take her to Manhattan by summer's end. The uncertainty made her stomach hurt. Lost in thought, Zoey pretended to read but watched the waves over the pages of her book instead, wondering why Dad hadn't texted her back. In the distance, a water skier in a bright orange vest wiped out on a turn. Zoey winced, remembering her own water tubing wipeout. The sleek white boat raced ahead, yanking the fumbling skier along until he finally managed to signal for the boat to slow down.

"The degree of that turn was way off," Isa commented, pursing her lips.

"Huh?" Zoey shot Isa a questioning look.

"The water skier," she answered quickly. "His knees weren't bent enough to make the turn. That's why he fell." Isa hugged her own knees to her chest. "I love water skiing. It's just like bowling."

Zoey was sure she'd heard wrong. "You water ski in the ocean. You bowl indoors. How are they the same?"

"Glad you asked," Isa said eagerly. She put her book down and grabbed a long string of seaweed from the sand.

"Becaaaaauuuuuse they're both about using angles, degrees, distance, and physics to achieve your goal! Say these are bowling pins," Isa said, drawing a triangle made out of ten dots in the sand. "To get a strike, you want to hit the space between the pin closest to you and the one closest behind it on the right at an angle of six degrees. . . ." Isa kept talking, but Zoey couldn't keep up. Isa was obviously a math whiz.

"You're making me wish I brought a protractor to the beach," Zoey joked when Isa came up for air.

"Oh. I bring mine everywhere!" Isa fished through her bag, tossing makeup, sunblock, and a graphing calculator on the sand.

Lacey groaned.

"Noooo. Put all that stuff away, Isa. Come on, save

it for your high school teachers. This is summer break!" Lacey flipped her sunglasses to the top of her head, rolling her eyes and scrunching her nose.

"High school teachers?" Zoey asked Isa.

"Genius here took geometry with the ninth grade last year," Lacey answered for Isa, still wrinkling her nose like Isa being smart was just as unappealing as Zoey's lackluster sense of style. She put her sunglasses on and lay back on her paisley pink towel.

Isa's bottom lip quivered. She bit it and stuffed her giant protractor and graphing calculator back into her purse, then crossed her arms over her chest and stared hard at the ocean. The girls lapsed into awkward silence. Lacey went back to reading on her phone, but clearly guilt was eating at her because Zoey kept catching her looking up.

"GEEZ, I didn't mean to insult your big brain. Sorry, Isa," Lacey said finally.

"What are you talking about?" Isa asked, turning a page primly in her library book. The plastic cover rustled as she smoothed it on her giant green towel, which was patterned with cheerfully bright lemons and watermelons. "Everything's fine."

"Ugh, stoooooop. Don't be like that," Lacey said, flipping her glasses back to the top of her head to eye Isa more closely. Isa ignored her, pretending to read.

"I'm sorry. How about I go get us fries?" Lacey said, poking Isa in the arm.

Isa shrugged a shoulder.

Lacey groaned loud enough for the twenty-something couple snoozing beneath their umbrella behind them to glance up in alarm.

"How about fries and chocolate shakes for all of us? I really *am* sorry," Lacey said, sounding contrite. This time, Zoey detected a note of real remorse in Lacey's tone.

Isa grinned. "All right, you're forgiven. And you don't have to buy me a milkshake," Isa said, then she giggled to herself like she'd just thought of a joke no one else was in on yet. Her braces gleamed in the sun. "But, I mean, I won't stop you either. Like, if you really waaant a chocolate shake and you don't want to drink alone, I don't mind having one too. . . ." She trailed off sweetly, still smiling.

"Haha, okay, I get it," Lacey said, grinning back. "Zoey, do you want one too?" she asked, getting up.

Zoey was surprised by the offer. "Um, no thanks," she said. Lacey shrugged before walking off to buy the shakes. When she was out of earshot, Zoey turned toward Isa. Before she could say anything though, Isa's phone started ringing.

Cupping the screen to reduce the sun's glare, Isa squinted at the caller ID and rolled her eyes.

"*Hola, Mami,*" she answered, then paused while her mom talked.

"I *told* you I was going to the beach with Lacey and Zoey." She paused again. "*Zoey.* I told you already about her—my new friend." Isa flashed a smile at Zoey and continued chatting seamlessly in Spanglish. "Yes, *la que tiene* the grandpa who owns the bowling center. Gonzo's. Gonzo's!" Isa glared up at the cloudless blue sky in exasperation. "*Gonzo's!*" she shouted again, earning a mean look from the forty-something-ish woman sunbathing nearby. "No—you can't talk. Don't call me again. I'll be home by seven. Don't call—"

Isa took the phone off her ear and exhaled in frustration.

"Is everything okay?" Zoey asked.

"My mom can get on my last nerve sometimes. It's not just that she's overprotective. But she can't hear me over the twins' screaming, so I have to repeat everything a thousand times, and then she hangs up on me and calls me back again so we can repeat the same conversation a thousand more times." Isa locked her phone and tossed it on her towel. "Sorry," she half-smiled at Zoey.

"No worries," Zoey said, trying to stomp down on the envious little voice inside that wished her mother could bug her like Isa's. "Who are the twins?"

"My brother and sister. They're two years old and double trouble delicious, but they take all my mom's attention. Ever since they were born, it's like she's always running after them. But then she'll suddenly remember she's supposed to worry about me too, and when she has one of those moments she just totally freaks out if she can't get ahold of me, so I can't ever forget to take my phone or leave the ringer off or my mother will send in the marines."

"It's sweet that she loves you so much though," Zoey couldn't resist pointing out.

"You're right," Isa said, sighing. Zoey watched her pick up her phone and text a quick GIF of a cat saying "I love you" to her mom. Zoey realized that was yet another one of the many things she missed about Mami—frequent, spontaneous affection. Saying "I love you" without a big reason. Sure, Dad and José told Zoey they loved her all the time—but more out of habit than anything else—when they said good night, or hung up the rare phone call.

"Were you going to say something before my mom called?" Isa asked.

"Oh yeah," Zoey said, remembering Isa's tiff with Lacey. "I wanted to tell you that being smart is a good thing. You should be really proud! Man, I wish my dad were a little better at math, like you. Then maybe he wouldn't lose money on his dreams, and we wouldn't have to move around so much."

Isa nodded, blushing slightly. "My dream is to work for NASA. Figure out how to sustain human population growth by colonizing Mars."

"Wow," Zoey said, supremely impressed. "That's . . . like, a lot of wow."

Isa laughed and started reapplying sunblock. "What's *your* dream?"

Zoey opened her mouth to answer, then closed it when she realized she didn't know what to say.

What did she want to study in college? What did she want to do when she grew up? Did she want to get married and have kids someday? Did she want to travel the world? Drink tea in London? Find her great-grandparents' old house in Cuba?

All Zoey had were question marks. She shrugged at Isa. "I guess I should figure that out one of these days."

6

Later that afternoon, after Zoey had said goodbye to Isa and Lacey and left the beach, she ventured farther down the boardwalk to locate the sandwich shop Isa had described. If the owners were as nice as Isa said, maybe they'd consider partnering with Poppy. She had to try. And fortunately, finding the restaurant turned out to be super easy.

Apparently, the Triple Threat Chicken Café was the most happening spot on the boardwalk. White holiday lights threaded through a thatched roof twinkled above the café's packed outdoor tables. Dance music blasted from outdoor speakers. Oldies. Salsa. Hip-hop. The music was as eclectic as the decor. The closer Zoey walked, the more intrigued she was by a line of life-size statues that formed a sort of entryway into the café. The statues were all cartoonish-looking chickens—frozen in different states of performance art. One chicken wore a tutu, its feet lifted in a delicate pirouette. Another sported a long white wig. Glasses slid down its beak, and the chicken looked as if it were about to deliver the key monologue in a Shakespeare play. Zoey's favorite chicken statue, though, had two feet of blue hair, wore head-to-toe sequins, and clutched a guitar in one wing and a microphone in the other. It looked like the lead singer in a band. And the way the other chickens were arranged around it made them look like they were boogieing to its jam.

Forget a bake sale, thought Zoey. Maybe what Poppy needed to get people's attention were dancing chickens. They made you want to stay and party and have fun. Bopping slightly to the beat of the hit song spilling from the ceiling speakers, Zoey pushed the door open and bumped into someone's shoulder.

"Sorry!" she exclaimed, losing her footing and starting to fall. A strong arm instantly caught her, stopping her from crashing through the glass.

"Careful there!" José said, letting go of Zoey's middle and shaking his head at her clumsiness.

"What are you doing here?" Zoey asked. She'd thought he was back at Gonzo's, still trying to fix the pinball machine.

José's lips drew together into a thin line, and he didn't answer right away. Zoey shot him a questioning glance, but José just stood there awkwardly next to a revolving case full of pies. Zoey's mouth watered, noticing a fudge cake dusted in chocolate sprinkles and drizzled in raspberry sauce. Her stomach grumbled. She should've taken up Lacey on that milkshake. Oh well. Maybe José would spring for a piece of cake. Or Zoey could buy herself a slice, she thought, remembering she had her bake sale cash on her. José jammed his hands in his pockets, and Zoey realized he wasn't eating or ordering or even playing on his phone. Just . . . standing there.

"What are you doing here?" Zoey asked again.

José put his hands in his pockets. "Hanging out."

Zoey squinted at him. Obviously, José wasn't telling her something. She glanced around the restaurant, pleased to find more dancing chicken statues inside. These were dressed like rock stars from different musical eras: A seventies disco queen held court beside the deli. A nineties boy band silently serenaded the kitchen doors. And a chicken statue bearing a suspicious resemblance to a current pop star took up residence by the restrooms. The café's plush red booths brimmed with customers.

Then Zoey noticed the girl with the long curly hair that José had been talking to the other day by the pinball machine, whizzing from table to table with a tray full of water glasses and soda cans.

"Ohhh. I get why you're 'hanging out' here." Zoey raised her eyebrows knowingly at her brother, making air quotes.

José's cheeks burned red.

"Hi there! You must be Zoey, José's sister," the girl said, pausing in front of them. "I'm Toni-Ann."

Zoey stared. "*You're* Toni-Ann? Oh my gosh! That's so funny."

"Zoey!" José's eyes widened in embarrassment.

"Oh," Zoey said quickly. "No. I don't mean *you're* funny because of anything José said. Like, he hasn't said anything about you! Not yet anyway," Zoey reassured.

"Zoey!" José barked again, glaring at her.

"Um, what I mean is, my friend Isa Levine suggested that I come here and talk to you," Zoey explained, desperate to clarify. "She said your restaurant makes the best sandwiches in the world, and that more people would probably come to our grandpa's bowling alley if they knew they could buy your food there. I tried running a bake sale today, but snacks weren't enough to get Poppy more customers."

José looked like he hoped the checkered floor would open up and swallow him whole.

"I think we need to get serious," Zoey said, pressing on. "I think we need chicken."

"Chicken has been known to save the day," Toni-Ann said, flashing a warm smile at José. "It sounds like a win-win for both our restaurant and the bowling alley. What do you think, José?"

José exhaled and smiled back. "I think so too," he said.

Zoey felt hope burst inside her like confetti. She had a good feeling about Toni-Ann. "Would you please talk to Poppy about partnering? He'll probably take you more seriously than me."

"Sure," Toni-Ann said. "I have to run it by my parents first, but I'm sure they'll be on board. Then I'll try to stop by within the next week or so to talk to your Poppy. Does that work?"

"Perfect." Zoey beamed. She felt lighter than she had since moving to the Jersey Shore.

"Okay, well, it's getting close to dinner. You don't want to ruin your appetite," José said, putting a hand on Zoey's shoulder and lightly spinning her toward the door. An egg-shaped clock above the dessert display ticked six o'clock.

"Aren't you coming?" Zoey asked, wiggling away from José and crossing her arms over her chest. "Poppy's making *your* favorite dinner tonight, *arroz con pollo* and *yucca con mojo*, remember?"

"I, ah, I thought I might stay and keep Toni-Ann company a little while longer," José said.

A family of seven walked in just then. The youngest two looked like identical twins. One ran straight to the pile of menus and knocked over the entire stack. The other climbed into a booth for two and immediately tried to pick up a knife. Toni-Ann snatched some crayons and paper mats from the hostess stand and dashed over to help the parents and usher them to a bigger table.

"I don't get off for another couple of hours," she called over her shoulder to José. "Go eat with your sister. Pick me up later. We can check out the movie with that superhero dude who travels through time to save Earth or whatever."

"You're literally the only human who hasn't seen this series. Get excited. I'm about to introduce you to the finest in cinematic artistry," José said.

"Robots exploding?" Toni-Ann squinted skeptically.

"Like I said, the *finest* in cinematic artistry."

"Mmm, 'kay. See you at nine."

Toni-Ann's smile was as big as José's when she turned back to take the next table's orders.

"So Toni-Ann, huh?" Zoey elbowed José in the ribs as they walked home in the early twilight. "She seems nice."

"She is," José agreed.

"And pretty. She has excellent fashion sense," Zoey tossed it out there. She was a big fan of the scarlet beaded maxidress Toni-Ann wore beneath her blue uniform apron emblazoned with the café's logo. "Maybe she can take me shopping sometime," she added.

"Okay, let's not get ahead of ourselves. Toni-Ann and I just met." José looked uncomfortable.

"So? She's nice. She's pretty. She has excellent fashion sense. *And* she wants to help us save Poppy's bowling alley."

"Yeah, okay, she seems really great," José admitted, in such a quiet, almost reverent voice that Zoey's own heart soared. It was the same tone Dad used to talk about Mami. Zoey had never heard José talk about his old girlfriends that way. Maybe Toni-Ann was The One. Zoey's mind raced with possibilities. Maybe her brother was falling so head-over-heels in love with Toni-Ann that he wouldn't go to college in Florida after all. Maybe he'd decide to stay!

"I'm glad you have a new girlfriend. I like seeing you happy," Zoey said, choosing her words carefully. She didn't want to freak José out.

"She's not my girlfriend, Zo."

"Not yet," Zoey pointed out.

José grunted—which Zoey interpreted to mean he did, in fact, hope Toni-Ann would become his girlfriend.

"New subject," he said. "Josh Hernandez texted me today."

"Josh Hernandez?"

"My new roommate at UF."

"Oh." Zoey had a funny feeling José was about to stomp on her heart like a piece of litter on the ground. "What'd he want?"

"To say hi, for starters. We just got our freshman dorm assignment. But then we started talking. He seems cool. He's from Gainesville, so he already knows the town inside out. And he wants to major in biomedical engineering. And, you know, I was leaning toward civil or electrical engineering. Biomedical never really crossed my mind. But I started researching it today after Josh texted. And now I'm thinking maybe the chance to work on medical technology might be a lot more interesting, you know? The application is so immediately relatable. I could help save people's lives. . . ." José talked on and on, gesturing with his hands, almost floating down the block in his excitement.

Zoey followed, her heart lying broken on the side-walk behind them as she realized Toni-Ann couldn't keep her brother in New Jersey any more than she could.

7

The next day, Isa, Lacey, Patrick, and Tyler returned to Gonzo's to prepare for the Summer Big Bowl Championship. They invited Zoey to practice with their team again. Patrick and Lacey focused almost exclusively on their own games, but Isa and Tyler were more interested in teaching Zoey how to bowl. Isa attempted to explain the wonders of geometry, and, though Zoey still didn't really understand the math, she did her best to eyeball and imitate the physical angles at which Isa showed her to stand, as well as to hold and release the ball at the right times. Tyler watched intently, critiquing Zoey's form. Soon the trio had Zoey's ball curving nicely when it whooshed down the lane. Zoey began to knock over a few pins each turn with increasing regularity, and found the hollow clattering sound they made as they fell to the floor oddly satisfying. Almost as good as the euphoria Zoey experienced when her soccer ball flew past the other team's goalie and into the net.

Unfortunately, Lacey hadn't bowled a single strike since they'd started playing at Gonzo's (though she always managed to knock over more pins than Zoey). And it was obvious she was pretty bitter about it.

"If you guys don't want to go back to the place with the strobe lights, you should try to get us permission to practice at the school bowling alley," Lacey complained to Patrick, twirling a long blond lock of hair nervously around her fingers. "I feel like my game is off here."

Tyler gave Zoey a knowing look. "Stop whining, Lacey."

Lacey's eyes blazed at Tyler.

"I'm not whining! It's the truth." She sucked in her cheeks and turned back to Patrick, tapping her foot. He sighed.

"Before we found Gonzo's, I tried getting permission to play at school over the summer," Patrick said. He stood up to select his favorite yellow ball from the rack. "But we can't. The school alley is booked solid for camp field trips, and they won't give us priority because the Summer Big Bowl Championship isn't officially part of the league we play in during the year."

"Fine." Lacey plopped down on the metal bench. She swung her legs back and forth and sulked, but she didn't say anything more until her ball rolled into the gutter again on her next turn.

"That's it! The arrows on the lane are too faded. My ball's going too slow because the floor is so scuffed up. This place is such a dump!" She shot each of her teammates a challenging look. "I'm not the only one whose game is off. Neither of you guys is playing as well as you usually do," she accused Patrick and Tyler. "Only Mrs. Math Genius over there—" Lacey pointed at Isa "—is rolling strikes."

"Hey, don't go insulting my game," Patrick said, checking the screen above. "I'm scoring just fine."

"Yeah, me too. You're just having a bad day and looking for excuses," Tyler piped in, shaking his head.

Zoey sat quietly in the corner, trying to disappear into the cold bench. Lacey freaking out about how she didn't want to bowl at her grandfather's alley felt like a double burn to Zoey. Like Lacey was both trying to convince the other kids not to be Zoey's friend and also trying to deprive Poppy of the business he so desperately needed. But glancing around the bowling alley, Zoey hated to admit that Lacey had a point. She'd thought the very same thing on her first day: Gonzo's was a lot shabbier than it had been before Abuela died. Beige paint peeled from the ceiling and along the walls. The lanes that used to gleam like freshly waxed cars had dulled to a dirty brown. Sure, José had finally fixed the pinball machine, but Skee-Ball, air hockey, and all the rest still bore yellow caution tape and out-of-service signs. This place *was* a dump, just like Lacey had said. The truth landed like a concrete block on Zoey's chest. But getting discouraged wouldn't solve anything. Like Mami always said, *Dale la vuelta*—turn it around. Whatever problem you're facing, spin it up, down, side to side, until you find the best way to fix it. And Zoey already knew what needed to be done here.

So she slipped away from the group to find Poppy. He was at the shoe rental counter, hunched over his computer and frowning at a spreadsheet.

"Poppy, where are the cleaning supplies?"

"Eh?" Poppy didn't look up.

"The cleaning supplies," Zoey repeated.

"What spilled? Where?" Poppy glanced over at Zoey's friends. It was Lacey's turn. Her expression was sour. She half-heartedly rolled her purple ball straight into the gutter again. Tyler gestured wildly with his hands, and Zoey could tell he was blaming Lacey for her own lackluster performance from the way Lacey crossed her arms defensively over her chest and marched halfway down the lane, pointing out every scuff mark with the toe of her bowling shoe.

Zoey squared her shoulders.

"No one spilled anything. I just think we need to clean up."

Poppy tsk-tsked.

"*Ay, mija.* Go play with your friends. *Muchas gracias,* but I don't need you to do housekeeping."

"But the place needs it," Zoey said, running a hand over the counter and showing Poppy the gray dust that stuck to the pads of her fingers.

Poppy sighed.

"I know, and I'll get to it, *mija.* One of these days. You have fun and let the adults work. *Créame,* believe me, you will have your whole life to work. Enjoy being a kid while you can."

Zoey opened her mouth to protest, but Tyler suddenly appeared behind her.

"Hey, Zoey, we were wondering what you wanted to do about lunch."

"I vote we stay here to squeeze in more practice and order pizza again," Patrick called as he and the girls walked over.

"No one cares what I think so I'm not even going to

mention the new hamburger place that just opened on Seagull Street," Lacey said, examining the bright red nail polish on her short fingernails.

"Good, because I'm not in the mood for burgers so I didn't hear anyone say anything about them," Tyler said pointedly.

Lacey pouted.

"Of course we care what you think," Isa said to Lacey, sounding exasperated. "But I'm kind of in the mood right now for pizza too."

Patrick smiled and pulled out his phone.

"Pizza it is!"

The group began debating toppings. Lacey pushed passionately for pineapple, but was outvoted yet again in favor of mushrooms and black olives.

"How about pineapple on just two slices?" Isa asked, striving for compromise. The boys agreed. Zoey didn't care what fruit or vegetables topped her pizza so she didn't weigh in. She turned back to Poppy, but he waved her off.

"Have fun with your friends, eh?" Poppy said meaningfully to Zoey, and disappeared with his laptop into the broom closet that doubled as his back office.

That night when José went with Toni-Ann to the mall and Poppy drove off to the grocery store, Zoey figured she had no choice but to sneak into Gonzo's and clean up on her own. It was weird being there in the dark, and eerie even though it wasn't that late. Outside, a steady stream of people sauntered past on the boardwalk, which was lit by tall lamps. Wisps of their conversation kept Zoey company after she decided to leave the front door propped open to let in some light so that she'd feel less alone.

Now where did Poppy hide his cleaning supplies, Zoey wondered. The only soap she could find was the pink antibacterial stuff in the bathroom dispenser. She dumped almost an entire dispenser's worth on the first two lanes and got to work using the Cuban mop and old blue towel she'd found under the desk in his office. But she'd only managed to scrub one lane down when she heard someone shouting for her outside.

"Zoey! *Mija*, are you here?"

The overhead lights suddenly turned on and Zoey blinked as her eyes adjusted to the light. When she could see, she saw Poppy standing at the end of the lane, arms crossed over his chest.

"What are you doing, *mija*? You scare me so bad! *Ay ay ay, un momento*," Poppy said, breathing hard, clutching his chest, and collapsing onto a bowling bench.

"Poppy!" Zoey dropped the wooden mop and hurried to sit next to him. "Are you okay?"

"No, I'm not okay! When I came home and saw you no there, I get worried!" Poppy exclaimed, waving his arms in the air. "Don't do this to me again. You go somewhere—you tell me or José first, *lo entiendes?*"

"Yes Poppy," Zoey said, swallowing hard. "I'm sorry. I didn't mean to scare you."

"Don't do it again," Poppy said, exhaling and running a hand through his thin gray hair. "I'm just glad you're okay. But *mija, qué estás haciendo aquí?*" He looked down at the towel covered in pink bathroom soap, and his jaw dropped.

"You came back to clean?" he asked disbelievingly.

Zoey nodded.

Poppy's eyes bugged out of his head. A muttered stream of Spanish words erupted from his mouth. When he at last finished, he said, "*Niña*, if you don't use the right products and equipment, you can ruin the floor! These are real wooden floors! Not that synthetic garbage like in *los* new bowling centers! You can't just use anything! What you use? Why it pink? Why you do this, *mija?* Explain yourself." Poppy's gaze was furious. Zoey had never seen him this upset with her before. He usually only got this worked up around Dad.

"I just…I thought if the alley was cleaner and looked nicer then maybe more customers would come. I don't want you to lose Gonzo's to Mr. Silos," Zoey whispered, trying not to cry.

"I told you, *mija*. That is my problem. I don't want you worrying about adult problems. You have your whole life to worry. I want you to have fun. This is summer!"

Zoey sighed, exasperated. "But I can't have fun knowing you might lose your dream. This bowling alley is everything to you," she said. All at once Poppy's shoulders sagged and his angry scowl turned into a sad frown. Zoey couldn't help thinking Poppy looked *really* old. Gray-haired and deflated. His short-sleeve, button-down shirt too baggy over his loose, wrinkly skin. All Zoey wanted to do was to give Poppy a hug and tell him everything would be okay. But increasingly, it seemed it wouldn't be. So Zoey stayed still, twisting her hands in her lap and wishing she could be like Isa or Lacey, only concerned about a bowling championship or what color to paint her nails, instead of constantly feeling like she was a cracked picture frame responsible for holding up her family, even though two of the most important loved ones in the photograph were gone.

"*Ay, mija*, you are so much like your mother," Poppy said, surprising Zoey. Most of the time, Zoey *wished* she was like her mother. Mami always knew what to do. She was beautiful and strong and capable. Zoey, on the other hand, was messy and insecure and tired of watching her well-intentioned plans crash and burn.

Poppy's lips curved into a grim smile at Zoey's doubtful expression.

"I mean it. And no as a compliment either, my little *jefa*. Your mami was always trying to help the people she loved. But going behind people's backs, keeping secrets, and telling lies—that's no really help, eh?" Poppy eyed Zoey knowingly, like he'd X-rayed her brain. "That just get you into trouble. And your mami always doing that with your dad. She keep all his failures a secret. She try to secretly clean them up with the wrong soap, like you. She no tell us they were having problems until it was too late. When you were getting evicted from your apartment or your dad lose his job again."

Poppy's jaw twitched. "Michael cause your mami so many problems. He is no a responsible man. He is *un*—"

"Tell me a story about Mami when she was a kid," Zoey interrupted softly. Even if he was right, it still hurt to hear Poppy speak badly about Dad. And he'd just finished criticizing Mami. Which was super strange. Usually Poppy talked about his daughter like she was as perfect as Zoey remembered. And yet the idea that her mother wasn't a hundred percent perfect—that she struggled the same way Zoey struggled now to help the people she loved—made Zoey feel weirdly better. Like she wasn't as alone, somehow.

Poppy's shoulders relaxed. He leaned back against the bench, sighing.

"*Ay ay ay*, your mami was the most stubborn person in the world. I remember one time she climb into a tree across the street—it no there anymore—but it was this *muy grande* oak tree, and she no come down. I tell her I going to throw out all her toys. She don't care. No dessert. She no care. No playing with her friends for a month. She no care. She not coming out of that tree! Okay, after dinner, I climb up the tree, I tell her, '*Pero que esta pasando, mija?* Why you want to live in this tree?' She tell me, 'Oh, Papi, I'm just collecting good dreams from the tree and the sky and the birds.'"

Poppy smiled fondly at Zoey. "I ask her, 'Why you want their dreams? You need to make your own dreams.' She told me it because she was having *pesadillas*, nightmares, about scary movies she'd watched at her friend's house. She'd climbed the tree to find better dreams to take to sleep with her. *Imaginate. Ay*, she was so sweet, *mija*. There she was, this little girl in a crown made out of yellow paper and a pink tutu, *tan linda mi princessa*. That night I gave her the blanket your abuela sewed for my birthday when we first got married that was on our bed. I told your mami, '*Mira*, look at the birds and the hearts and all the happy symbols your mom,' *bueno*, your abuela"—Poppy clarified for Zoey—"'weave into this blanket. It represents all her good hopes and dreams for our marriage and future, and now this blanket gonna protect you and give you good dreams when you go to sleep.'"

Zoey smiled. Mami had told her the same story when she'd given Zoey the blanket in first grade when she'd been having nightmares about a bloody ghost. The kids at school had tried summoning one in the bathroom mirror during lunch, but none had come, and Zoey feared maybe the summons *had* worked, but the clever evil spirit had immediately hidden away. Maybe the bloody ghost was planning to pop out at her when she least expected it and kidnap her in the middle of the night. A cast of Halloween horrors had haunted her dreams for weeks after that, until Mami gave her the blanket. Zoey had slept, ghost-free, with the blanket ever since.

"That blanket is on my bed now," she informed Poppy. "I love it when you tell me stories about Mami when she was little. Did she always want to be a chef?"

"Ooof, *ay, sí*," Poppy said, chuckling. "Though I think

at first your mami should be a lawyer. She always like to talk. And to argue. *Ay ay ay.* She gave your abuela a hard time, especially when she was a teenager. She fight with your abuela about everything—her clothes, the boys we no let her go out with, the parties she want to go to, her curfew, her diet. She always trying some new diet she didn't need and cooking new recipes. She argue at home. She argue at school. She was a debate champion," Poppy reminisced, smiling proudly.

"She won trophies. I remember one time she research the dangers of smoking for a debate competition. Then she convince me to quit my cigars. She was so happy. I tell her, 'You should be a lawyer.' She say, 'No, I always want to be a chef!' I say, '*Perfecto*, even better, you come work here in Gonzo's with me. Help Abuela with the café. This business is for you.' '*Pero no,*' she tell me, 'I will not stay home to cook rice and beans my whole life! I want more flavors.' And she not just talking about the food. She marry your dad after she go to culinary school, and you know the rest. But yes, your mami always, always wanted to be a chef. Ever since Abuela teach her to cook here in Gonzo's when she was a little girl."

"I guess José is like Mami, always knowing what he wanted to do. He's always wanted to be an engineer,"

Zoey said, biting her lip. It seemed the only person in her immediate family who dreamed of being more than just one thing was her dad, and Zoey wasn't sure anymore she wanted to grow up to be like him. Not if it meant leaving behind the people she loved.

"Was the bowling alley always your dream, Poppy?" she asked, fearing she already knew the answer. "Like, even when you were a kid in Cuba?"

"No, in Cuba I thought I wanted to be a doctor," Poppy said, stunning Zoey. "But we couldn't afford for me to go to medical school when we come to this country, so my dream change here."

"Why'd you want to run a bowling alley?" Zoey asked, realizing she had no idea why Poppy ever opened Gonzo's.

"*Bueno*, a few reasons," Poppy said, holding out his hand like he was about to tick the reasons off on his fingers. "But the most important one is my own dad, he, ah, how you say, *an ingeniero*, an engineer—like what José want to do—when he in Cuba. But when we come here, the only job he can find is to be the janitor in a bowling alley."

"Did he work in *this* one?"

"Yes," Poppy said, his lips curving up in pride. "I buy it from the original owner, but that take a long time.

First, my dad work here, then he get me a job working here too. I was the waiter. That's how I meet your abuela."

"Really?" Zoey said. "But I always thought you'd met reaching for the last piece of chocolate cake in a bakery. Mami used to joke that's why we all inherited such a sweet tooth."

Poppy laughed and tsked at the same time, waving his hand in a dismissive gesture.

"*Ay*, I know, your mami change the story when she want to be fancy, pretend her father and grandfather were no poor immigrants who work as janitors and waiters. But the truth is I was working as the waiter here in the bowling alley café when your abuela come in with her friends to bowl and have lunch. Actually, I notice her *friend* first," Poppy said, chuckling.

"What?!"

"Yes, I send the friend a piece of chocolate cake, on the house. And your abuela, she noticing Henry—the other waiter!" Poppy chuckled again, though Zoey still didn't see what was so funny about her grandparents not living the love-at-first-sight fairy tale she'd always ascribed to them. It was too weird thinking of her grandparents as teenagers around José's age, even temporarily interested in dating people who weren't each other.

"So, Henry and I, we invite the girls to bowl a game with us after our shift end and you know what? I don't even remember the friend's name, but she boring as a potato. A potato! And I notice your abuela not only is she very beautiful, even *more* pretty than her friend, but she sweet and smart and funny too. We stay talking so long, everybody else leave. I have the key to lock up so is no problem, except her father, Bernardo, show up. *El bombero*," Poppy said respectfully.

"The bomb maker?" Zoey was appalled. "My great-grandfather was a bomb maker?"

Poppy stared at her like she'd just grown a second nose.

"What? *¡Claro que no, niña!* We need to teach you better Spanish as soon as possible," he grumbled, shaking his head. "I should start quizzing you again like I do when you were younger! *Bombero* means firefighter. You know, with the hat and the hose? Bernardo was a firefighter. And man, was your *bisabuelo* scary. Especially when he was mad. He more than six feet tall, with big, beefy arms, *y ya tu sabes* what he must have been thinking because his daughter no home and out with some guy she just meet. I thought he was going to kill me. But he calm down when he realize we were just having the time of our life talking until two a.m., your abuela and I," Poppy said, his eyes twinkling. He looked at the spot where the Skee-Ball machine sat broken.

"We were talking right over there. Back then, that was the part of the bowling alley you can buy ice cream. I remember we share a few scoops of pistachio. I fall in love with your abuela that night, and I think she start to fall for me too because we never apart after that until ..."

Poppy sighed, and Zoey could tell he meant to say until her abuela passed away. She was sad, but relieved Poppy's version of events preserved the pristine meant-to-be heart of her grandparents' love story that she'd always treasured, even if it turned out she'd had the details all wrong.

"So when did you buy Gonzo's?" Zoey asked curiously.

"Ah, that was a few years later. The original owner, his name Mr. Bowman, he want to retire and move to Florida. Your abuela and I had just got married. I have a little bit saved. She help me sweet talk the bank to give us a mortgage so we can pay the rest and buy the bowling alley from Mr. Bowman. Back then you don't have *tanto papeleo*, so much paperwork, like today. I try refinancing a few months ago and *tsk*," Poppy tut-tutted. "So much *papeleo* nowadays. I don't get through. *Bueno*, here we are."

"I want to help save your dream, Poppy," Zoey said, gazing earnestly at him.

"I know, my little *jefa*, I know," Poppy said, sighing and patting Zoey's hand. The two were quiet, each lost in their own thoughts.

After a moment, Poppy said, "But you know what? I think, over time, my dream change again. When I look back on my life, it feels more like you—and José and your mami—were my real dream, the dream I didn't even know I wanted when I was a little boy in Cuba. I didn't realize my kids would become my real legacy, my biggest dream come true." Poppy glanced around Gonzo's and frowned like he was seeing its scuffed floors and walls for the first time. He shook his head.

"It's good that this place isn't my only dream, eh? Since it's falling apart." He laughed, but the laugh sounded forced, and Zoey knew Poppy cared a lot more about losing Gonzo's to Mr. Silos than he let on. She didn't want to upset him though, so Zoey changed the subject.

"I don't know what my dream is yet," she said lightly. She thought of Dad and his constant moving. "And I'm afraid of not figuring it out and bouncing from one thing to another that never works out." Then she also thought of José and his single-minded college essays. "But also, how do I pick just *one* dream?"

Poppy gave Zoey a hug.

"You take your time. *Tomate tu tiempo, mija,*" he whispered into her ear. "The world is full of dreams, and you are young. *No te apresures.* There's no need to rush."

8

The next day was slow again at the bowling alley. Actually, Zoey thought, slow was too generous of a description. Not a single customer set foot inside Gonzo's. So she was thrilled when Isa's texts popped up on her phone, interrupting the random stream of You-Tube videos about sports and baking that Zoey watched for lack of better options. Apparently, Lacey had found a new bowling alley for the team to try tomorrow. Zoey was invited to their practice, as well as to a small slumber party at Lacey's house tonight. And as bad as Zoey felt about Poppy losing her new friends as customers, she was excited to have been included in the sleepover.

At least she was, until Poppy dropped Zoey off in front of the most intimidating house she'd ever seen. A local theme park could easily have fit atop the rolling green lawn that stretched between Lacey's front door and the tall metal gate Poppy drove through after pressing buttons on an intercom. Big as a museum and built from raw gray and beige stones, the mansion reminded Zoey of a storybook castle. Ornate trellises and colorful flower boxes spilled from every window on the second and third floors. Turrets even lined the roof.

When Zoey knocked, she half expected a drawbridge to fall at her feet. Instead, a housekeeper in a starched blue uniform took Zoey's sleeping bag and disappeared down a marble-tiled hallway, leaving Zoey alone in the living room. She clutched the backpack with her toothbrush and change of clothes and willed herself not to freak out. Unfortunately, the decor inside Lacey's house seemed to be culled from Zoey's worst nightmares.

Copper statues in sharp, pointy shapes rose at various heights from a white plush carpet thick as quicksand, and canvases covered in splotches of green and black paint that reminded Zoey of thickly tangled vines hung from the walls. Zoey liked the deep emerald hue and velvety fabric the couches were upholstered in, but the lack of cushions and narrow frame didn't make them look very comfortable to sit on. Zoey almost fell over a small white statue of a crouching lion beside the doorway that blended into the carpet. The lion looked, upon closer inspection, like it was ready to pounce. She backed away from it slowly.

"Come on in!" A blond, blue-eyed woman who looked like Lacey-in-thirty-years emerged from a door Zoey hadn't noticed earlier on the opposite end of the room. Beside her yapped a tiny terrier in a ruffled gingham vest.

"You must be Zoey! I'm Heather, Lacey's mom. So nice to meet you. Don't be shy," she said when Zoey hesitated awkwardly in the doorway, afraid to walk past the dog, which kept sniffing at her ankles.

Zoey breathed through her nose, reminding herself she was much bigger than the dog, and that if Lacey's family could afford designer clothes for a pooch, they'd probably also invested in training their beloved pet not to bite guests.

"Come. Follow me. The girls are outside by the pool," Heather said, leading the way.

Zoey smiled nervously, smoothed her frizzy ponytail, and did her best to ignore the dog, which lost interest in her as soon as she failed to reciprocate its attention and began barking at Heather instead.

"Who's a good boy? Who's Momma's beautiful boy? Who's my sweet Windsor?" Heather cooed. She scooped the pup into her arms, and Zoey couldn't help noticing how well he completed her outfit. Lacey's mom wore strappy heels beneath scarlet yoga pants and a tennis bracelet that sparkled distractingly in the late afternoon sun when they stepped out onto the family's expansive patio.

"Zoey!" Lacey and Isa both hopped off cushioned wicker recliners, careful not to spill their fruity drinks with little umbrellas in them. They put their cups down on a small glass table laden with sparkling water, berries, and a giant tray of cheese. Then the girls hugged and air-kissed Zoey's cheeks like they hadn't just seen her yesterday.

"Hey, guys!" Zoey tried to match their enthusiasm, still feeling unsure of herself but attempting to hide it. "Your house is amazing!"

"Thanks," replied Lacey airily.

"Have fun, ladies. Don't play your music too loud. And don't forget to change. We're going out to dinner at seven," Lacey's mom called over her shoulder as she shut the sliding glass door and went inside.

"I didn't realize we were going out," Isa said. Rare worry lines appeared on her forehead. Isa took a big gulp of smoothie and glanced down at her sequined tank top and jeans shorts like they'd just called her a nasty name. "I didn't bring any nice clothes."

"Neither did I," Zoey said. If Isa was worried about *her* outfit (which looked plenty fancy to Zoey), then what should Zoey do? In her old jeans and hand-me-down soccer jersey, Zoey had dressed for dinner worse than Lacey's dog.

Lacey's lime green painted nails waved grandly through the air. "Don't worry. You guys can borrow a couple of dresses from me."

Isa exhaled, visibly relieved to have averted a fashion crisis. The creases on her forehead disappeared. "Ooo, can I borrow your high-neck halter dress with the tiered hem that kind of floats down to the knees? The one you wore to my bat mitzvah? It's, like, Tinker Bell chic. I looove that dress."

"You mean the green and purple one?"

"Yes!" Isa squealed.

"Sure." Lacey smiled.

"What kind of dress do you want to borrow?" she asked, turning to Zoey. "Do you like A-line, empire-waist, high-low, or are you not into dresses at all and more into wide-cut trousers?"

"Umm . . ." Zoey faltered. Ever since meeting Lacey and Isa, she'd started furtively pining online for clothes she couldn't afford, but her fashion vocabulary was still seriously lacking. "I guess just something that fits. I'm a lot taller than you."

The smile faded from Lacey's face. She looked at

Zoey like she was some tedious extra credit homework assignment not worth the bother.

"Maybe Zoey could borrow your striped royal blue maxi?" Isa piped in, consulting Lacey like Zoey wasn't standing right there. "It's long and stretchy, so it won't matter if the dress is a little short on her because of the height difference. And the color will probably go great with Zoey's dark hair."

Lacey nodded.

"Awesome. Thanks!" Isa exclaimed, thanking Lacey on Zoey's behalf, while Zoey stood there feeling dumb.

"No problem." Lacey relaxed back into her recliner and lazily slipped her phone out of her pocket.

"Ugh. I'm so bored with my hair," she said, using the selfie screen on her phone as a mirror. "But I don't want to change the color again. Do you think I could pull off an Ariana Grande ponytail?"

Lacey glanced questioningly from Isa to Zoey.

"Definitely." Isa sounded excited. "You want to try to do one tonight?"

"I don't *knoooow*," Lacey said. "Maybe it's too tall for me. What do you think, Zoey?"

"Um . . ." Zoey wished she could Google Ariana Grande's hairdo. But Lacey and Isa were both staring at her, awaiting an opinion.

"I, uh, I'm not sure what her hair looks like," Zoey finally confessed.

"WHAT? How do you not know Ariana?" Lacey looked personally affronted. She stared at Zoey as if she'd just admitted to farting in front of the Queen of England.

"I mean, I think I, uh, heard her songs once." Zoey's cheeks flamed. She wondered if Lacey was really rich and connected enough to be on a first-name basis with the pop star, or if this was just how normal people talked about celebrities.

"Look, here's a picture of the ponytail. It's kind of like her signature look." Isa helpfully shoved her phone under Zoey's nose.

"Oh, it's, ah, cute. Yeah. I like it," Zoey mumbled. "You should totally do your hair like that, Lacey." Lacey shrugged and continued gawking at Zoey. Isa clicked through to the next slideshow on the Hollywood gossip site she'd pulled up.

"LACE! Did you hear that Jake Idaho eloped with Maria Mendez?"

"No way! Ahhh, he's so cute! He has, like, the most gorgeous hazel eyes I've ever seen," Lacey said, whipping out her own phone to catch up on the scoop and making heart eyes at the link she found.

"Awwwww. They were on vacay in Scotland, and he just, like, wrote her a song on the spot, asking Maria to marry him! The single's going to drop later this year. Oh my gosh, they had the wedding in an abandoned castle. *Look* at that dress. A hundred percent lace with pearl trim and sequined rose petals on the bodice. I'm dying."

Isa gasped. "And Jake's going to guest star on her show!" she shouted, speed-reading on her phone. "He's going to play an ex-boyfriend who swoops into town to give Luke competition for prom king."

Prom king? Zoey didn't recognize the actors that Lacey and Isa were so worked up about and she didn't really care to find out more about them, but that last nugget made her curious.

"How old are these people?" she asked. "They got married in high school?"

"Noooo, they're in their twenties in real life, but they play teenagers on this high school show," Isa explained.

"Ohh." Zoey felt stupid. Again.

Lacey looked at Zoey like she wanted to ask if she came from Mars. Isa slurped the last of her pink fruity drink with the little umbrella.

"I'm running to the bathroom. Be right back."

Once Isa disappeared into the house, awkward silence descended between Zoey and Lacey.

To avoid Lacey's sharp gaze, Zoey stared straight ahead at the Olympic-size pool. It had infinity edges, so the water seemed to flow forever, nearly indistinguishable from the brilliant blue sky above. Yet another enchanted wing of this storybook castle, Zoey mused. She'd never seen a pool like theirs. She wished she could dive in and take her chances with whatever magical mischief lay beneath that enticingly smooth surface. It didn't matter that she didn't like the water—she would have done anything to never have to deal with Lacey or her judgy, scrunched-up nose again. To be honest, Zoey wasn't even sure why Lacey had invited her over in the first place.

When she couldn't take the awkwardness anymore, Zoey snapped, "What?"

"I just, like . . ." Lacey trailed off, still staring and sighing at Zoey. "I just don't *get* it."

"Get *what?*" Zoey watched Lacey warily.

"Why Tyler and Patrick talk to you so much? You don't know *anything*. Didn't they have bowling or fashion or even TV in Miami or wherever you came from?"

Zoey glared at her. Lacey was so *rude*. And the worst part was that Zoey didn't even think Lacey was trying to be rude. She genuinely thought Zoey was a freak.

"Hey! I might not know how Ariana wears her hair, but at least I don't have to worry about people only liking me for my money!" Zoey spit back, though she hadn't even realized how rich Lacey was until this afternoon. It made sense now though. Why the other team members put up with Lacey's whiny, spoiled attitude.

"That's not true!" Lacey said.

"Do you really think Isa would want to hang out with you if you weren't lending her fancy dresses for dinner and buying her chocolate milkshakes at the beach?"

Lacey's eyes blazed with rage, and her bottom lip trembled. She looked like she couldn't decide whether to cry or insult Zoey again or maybe just slap her in the face. But before she could say anything, her mom returned to the patio and shooed them both inside to change for dinner.

The rest of the night flew by under a phony halo of politeness. When Lacey returned from getting changed, her face was a blank slate with no trace of hurt or tears. Isa could tell something was up and kept asking if they were all right, but both Zoey and Lacey insisted everything was fine. Luckily, Lacey's older sister had just come home from college and dinner conversation revolved around her. Then, faking a stomachache, Zoey pretended to go straight to sleep the second they got back to Lacey's mansion. But she couldn't fall asleep, not really. She already regretted how mean she'd been, even if what she'd said was true. Her cramps had gotten better over the last few days, but she almost preferred them to the guilt that was eating away at her now. At dawn, Zoey crept out to the patio to ask José to pick her up early.

She was about to send the text when Isa snuck up on her.

"Are you trying to catch the sunrise?"

Zoey jumped so high she nearly fell in the pool.

"Oh, uh, n-n-no," Zoey stammered. "I was just about to call my brother for a ride home. Stomach still hurts. Ouch." She patted her belly.

Isa gave her a skeptical, probing look. "Come on. I know you and Lacey had a fight."

Zoey's temper flared instantly. The thought of Lacey badmouthing her to Isa really got under her skin.

"Did she tell you she started it? And that she hurt my feelings too?" Zoey said, outraged that Lacey must have given Isa a totally one-sided version of what happened. So unfair! Especially when *Lacey* was the one who'd been low-level mean to Zoey since the first day they'd met. Okay, maybe she'd been nicer when they went to read at the beach. But she'd been snooty all the other times! And last night was the very first time Zoey had ever snapped back!

"She didn't say anything. I can just tell," Isa said, folding her arms over her sparkly pink pajama top.

"Oh." Zoey looked down at her fuzzy frog slippers.

"So, do you want to tell me what happened?" Isa plopped down on a wicker recliner and beckoned for Zoey to sit in the seat beside her.

Zoey groaned, flopping onto the chair.

"I might've said something . . . ," Zoey said, pausing to breathe in through her nose and out through her mouth. She suddenly felt queasy as she recalled what she'd said to Lacey. "Well, something sort of unfair to Lacey because she basically called me boring, and she said she didn't know why Patrick and Tyler waste their time talking to me," Zoey confessed, realizing as she glossed over her part just how untrue her accusation had been: Isa obviously wasn't the type of person to choose friends based on finances. After all, Zoey was broke. And since their first encounter in the bathroom, Isa had shown Zoey kindness over and over again. Even when Zoey didn't deserve it.

Zoey's shoulders slumped. Her fake stomachache was certainly becoming more real.

"But I shouldn't have said what I did. I was mean, and what I said wasn't true. And I'm sure Lacey doesn't want me to go bowling with you guys today. So I'll just go home anyway," Zoey said, turning away to unlock her phone and text José.

"What? No, stop," Isa said. "Don't go home. When Lacey wakes up, just talk this out with her. Honestly, Lacey's probably just jealous of you."

"Jealous of *me?*" Zoey glanced up doubtfully at the turrets topping Lacey's mansion. How could anyone like Lacey with a family fortune and a closet full of the latest fashions envy Zoey in her hand-me-down T-shirts?

"Yeah. I'll tell you a secret, but you have to swear you won't repeat it," Isa said, looking through the glass patio door to make sure no one else was coming outside.

"Okay," Zoey said curiously.

Isa leaned closer, speaking in a hushed tone lest the hibiscus bush overhear.

"Lacey has a *huge* crush on Tyler, but she doesn't think he sees her as more than just a friend. She's probably jealous that you guys hit it off so quickly."

Huh. And here Zoey had thought Lacey's crush was on handsome, mysteriously serious Patrick. She wondered *why* someone as pretty and stylish as Lacey would go for a chubby, messy guy like Tyler. Then she immediately felt bad for judging based on appearances. Tyler was friendly and sweet. Totally crush-worthy. If not Zoey's type, personally.

"I mean, Tyler and I are just friends. There's nothing for Lacey to be jealous of."

"So then stay!" Isa said. "Just apologize to Lacey for whatever you said, and she'll probably apologize back. I know she comes across a little shallow at first, but I've been friends with Lacey a long time—since kindergarten. She has a good heart. You can fix this. I mean, you don't just go running off whenever things get hard, do you?" Isa asked, rhetorically. Like the answer was so clearly "no" that she didn't expect Zoey to disagree.

"Oh, um, yeah, you're right," Zoey replied, wondering if that was what Dad did. Quit every job and business the second it got hard. He still hadn't texted her back, and she'd messaged him three more times since her failed bake sale. When he'd left for his new job selling motorcycles in Manhattan, Zoey had been mad at him. Had Dad stuck her in the "too hard to bother with" category?

The possibility hurt to think about, but strengthened Zoey's resolve to take Isa's advice and work things out with Lacey. She definitely didn't want to handle things the way Dad was.

Zoey and Isa climbed the grand spiral staircase that grew like Rapunzel's tower from the corner of Lacey's enchanted forest of a living room. Every step was agony as Zoey worried about what she'd say to Lacey. In the bedroom, Lacey was now awake, sitting up in her four-poster bed, its frame shaped like a horse-drawn carriage. With a reassuring smile from Isa, Zoey marched over and took a deep, steadying breath. "I'm sorry for what I said by the pool yesterday. It was mean and not true," she apologized, the words coming out all in a rush.

Lacey looked at her thoughtfully before turning back her covers and standing up. She stared at Zoey for a long moment before saying, "I'm sorry too. Let's start over, okay?"

Then, to Zoey's surprise, Lacey *hugged* her! Zoey let out the breath she'd been holding, hugging Lacey back.

"I'd like that," Zoey said. From over Lacey's shoulder, Zoey saw Isa giving her two thumbs up.

When Lacey stepped back she smiled and said, "I'm starving. Who wants breakfast?" And then she disappeared out the door. Isa laughed and followed her. Zoey hung back for a moment though, still amazed at how easily Lacey had forgiven her. What if it could be that easy for her family? What if her Poppy just said he was sorry and hugged it out with Dad? What if José let the past go and told Dad he wanted to start over? But then another thought dawned on Zoey. What about Dad? Maybe he owed an apology, too. Zoey grabbed up her cell phone from by her sleeping bag—still no texts from him. Yes, he owes *me* an apology, Zoey decided, then pocketed her phone and ran to catch up with her friends.

Downstairs, Lacey's dad made chocolate chip pancakes from scratch in their enormous, light wood kitchen. The smell alone deposited Zoey in the stratosphere. When she took a bite, the taste catapulted her the final stretch to the moon. By the time they needed to get ready to meet Tyler and Patrick at the new bowling alley, the girls were all smiles. Lacey even showed Zoey how to put on eye shadow. Zoey felt grown-up and if not beautiful, then something approaching pretty, in the borrowed navy powder that clung subtly to her upper lash line, making her brown eyes look larger than usual.

Unfortunately, the new bowling alley was amazing. Clean and shiny and *busy*. Everything Poppy's bowling alley needed to be, but wasn't. Zoey tried not to dwell on it, but it was hard not to resent the bustling and fully functional arcade where they killed time playing air hockey and laser games while waiting for a lane to open up. Finally, after forty-five minutes, one did.

"You never have to wait for a lane at Gonzo's," Zoey couldn't help mentioning to Patrick, whispering so Lacey wouldn't overhear. "That's almost a whole hour of practice time you lost today."

He frowned, nodding seriously. Zoey turned away so he wouldn't see her smile, silently congratulating herself for putting Poppy's alley back in the running for future practice sessions. She glanced around the new bowling alley, noting the average customer was around their age. The group of guys next door in lane seven wore matching green tees. She wondered if they were competing in the Summer Big Bowl Championship too, and asked Tyler.

Tyler frowned when he spotted the guys in green shirts. "The Lightning Strikers. They actually won last year."

"They have a team name?" Zoey asked, surprised.

"Yeah, a super boring, cliché one," Tyler scoffed. "Lightning strike. Bowling strike. So ... *expected*."

"Does your team have a name? How come I haven't heard it before?"

Tyler laughed. "Because we couldn't agree. We chose our team name out of a plastic cup with everyone's suggestion written on a folded piece of paper inside. The winner was Isa's."

"What is it?"

"The Curve Breakers," Isa answered for Tyler, walking up to them. "Get it? Because we're A-plus bowlers, above the curve, and also because the best bowlers know how to manipulate angles and curves. A totes *brilliant* name, if I do say so myself!"

"Meh," Tyler shrugged, and Isa poked an elbow in his ribs.

"Whatever," he said, playfully batting her elbow away. "I liked the Whizzes, like a play on how the ball whizzes down the lane and we're smart whizzes who bowl the best. But Isa and Lacey thought Whizzes would make people think of peeing," Tyler said grumpily.

"It kind of does," Zoey said, laughing. "Sorry, Ty."

"Patrick!" the tallest and blondest of the Lightning Strikers shouted, noticing Zoey and her friends.

Patrick looked up and when he saw who'd called his name, he sucked in his breath and stood up straighter. The expression on his face made it clear Patrick wished he hadn't run into this guy, even as he gave him a friendly fist bump. Close to six feet tall and broader than any eighth grader she'd ever seen before, the blond guy reminded Zoey of a Viking. She could easily picture him in an iron helmet, setting sail from some snowy, seafaring town a thousand years ago to conquer the Atlantic.

"Hey there, Eric." Patrick forced a smile. "What's up?"

Ignoring Patrick's question, Eric the Viking (as Zoey privately nicknamed him) glanced past Patrick at his friends. His eyes lingered on Lacey, Isa, and Zoey.

"Lots of girls on your team this year, huh?"

Patrick shrugged, acknowledging as much.

"Too bad."

"Excuse me?!" Lacey, Isa, and Zoey exclaimed in unison. Beside them, Patrick and Tyler tensed.

"I just mean, you know, sports usually aren't coed because guys are so much better than girls. It isn't fair for them to compete in the same league," Eric the Viking said, smirking.

"You gotta be kidding," Lacey said.

"Yeah," Tyler jumped in. "Our best player is Isa, and she's a girl."

"All I'm saying is no chick from the WNBA competes with the guys in the NBA Finals," Eric said. Then he leaned down leisurely to steal a sip from Zoey's soda next to the screen keeping track of the scores.

"Hey, don't be such a jerk!" Isa yelled, but Eric was already heading back over to his friends. Zoey stared at the back of his head, her blood boiling. It took all her self-control to not snatch up the cup and go pour it down the back of Eric's shirt. That soda had cost three bucks, and she couldn't afford to replace it after failing to recoup most of her savings on the ill-fated Gonzo's bake sale.

"Don't worry. We'll show him," Patrick promised,

gritting his teeth. Zoey wasn't sure if he was talking to himself or the girls.

In the lane beside them, Eric picked up a sleek orange bowling ball and tossed it into the air like it was a basketball before catching it smoothly, rolling a perfect strike, and returning to a series of smug high-fives and laughs from his pals.

"Anyone can do that," Patrick called out loud enough for Eric to hear.

"Oh yeah?" Eric raised a lazy eyebrow at him in challenge. "You do it then."

Patrick's fingers clenched around the canary yellow bowling ball he'd just picked up.

"Your ball looks like Big Bird, so sure, I'll believe it can fly," Eric taunted.

"Seriously? Is that the best insult you can come up with?" Lacey called. "Everyone knows Big Bird doesn't fly!"

Patrick glanced back at the rack behind them. Zoey guessed he was thinking about choosing another ball in a less remarkable hue. But then he squared his shoulders and marched up to the foul line instead. It seemed he'd decided to own his bright yellow color choice, and Zoey was proud he hadn't given in to Eric's bullying.

But then Patrick tossed his bowling ball a couple of inches into the air and caught it.

"We're going to win this thing. Easy," Patrick vowed, talking to his team but staring straight ahead.

"Dude, you know that's not actually a basketball, right?" Lacey said.

"Don't show off," Isa said, shooting Eric some serious side-eye. "It's not worth it."

"Actually that ball looks more like the candy my nana used to keep in her purse," Eric called in a teasing tone, ignoring Isa and focusing on Patrick. "Tasted like lemon and honey. Good for sore throats."

"I have the best team in New Jersey. There's nothing anyone on any team can do that we can't do better," Patrick declared, eyeing his teammates, but still speaking loudly so that the Lightning Strikers would overhear. He tossed the ball again, higher. But this time it was at a weird angle.

The rest all happened so fast. The ball came plummeting down and Patrick dove to catch it out of reflex. But he slipped on the gleaming, slick wood floor, falling hard. Patrick yelped in pain as the ball landed a second later, clipping his fingers. Zoey and the others immediately rushed forward as behind them, Zoey heard the other team chuckling.

"Are you okay?" Isa asked.

"What were you thinking, dude?" Tyler said.

Breathing heavily, Patrick slowly stood up. The index finger on his right hand was bent the wrong way and his middle and ring fingers were quickly swelling and turning a dark shade of purple. His face crumbled as he looked down at his hands. Patrick whimpered, biting the inside of his cheeks. His eyes glistened, and Zoey could tell he was doing his best not to cry.

A moment later, a man and woman wearing employee shirts showed up. "Someone saw him fall and came to get us," the man said. "Are you all right?"

"My fingers. I think they're broken," Patrick gasped, squeezing his eyes in pain.

"You don't know that for sure," Tyler said softly.

"I broke my index finger before," he said haltingly. "I remember what it felt like. I know. And this time it might be more than one." Grimacing, he tried to wiggle his phone out of his pocket with his left hand, but stopped abruptly, letting out a groan. "I'll tell you the number. Can someone please call my dad to come pick me up? Practice is over for today."

9

The next morning Zoey was stunned to find every member of the Curve Breakers—even Patrick—waiting to greet her outside Gonzo's.

"You kids are the first customers I have in a while who get up to bowl when we open at nine a.m.," Poppy said, sounding impressed. He lifted the metal shutter and unlocked the front door. "Come on in."

"How're you feeling?" Zoey asked, eyeing the new splint on Patrick's index finger and the tape wrapped around the other two fingers.

"Awful," Patrick said. He glared down at his hand like it had just abandoned him on an old-timey battlefield as the enemy's trumpet sounded. "Thankfully, only one is broken but the other two are badly sprained and I'm not allowed to move them. I can't bowl like this. And I've never been able to knock down a single pin with my other hand. I'm out."

He stared down at the floor dejectedly.

"I'm so sorry," Zoey said. She knew how much playing in the championship meant to him.

He exhaled heavily. "I should never have let Eric get in my head like that. I've put the whole team in jeopardy." But then he looked up at her.

"Zoey, we need you to please fill in at the championship for me," Patrick said.

Everyone nodded and Zoey took a step back, overwhelmed.

"What? Me? But I'm not a good bowler," Zoey protested.

"You're not. Not yet anyway. But it doesn't matter. You're literally the *only* person who could fill in. The fifth member of our team in our school league is at sleepaway camp until August," Patrick said, looking down at his splint and closing his eyes.

"And you *are* a good bowler," Isa said, aiming a pointed look at Patrick.

Isa then smiled encouragingly at Zoey. "You've improved so much since the first day we met. Plus, I can give you more tips!"

"So can I," Tyler said, rallying. "Please. We need you."

"We really do," added Lacey, swallowing hard like she was trying not to cry. "We'll have to forfeit if we don't have four bowlers. Mr. Martin was really strict when he drew up his summer championship rules. And we've worked so hard already. Please do it, Zoey."

Zoey sat down on the bench and started massaging her forehead, wishing she could rub hard enough to smooth down all the conflicting thoughts running through her brain. The last thing she needed was another problem on her plate. Did she have the time to figure out a way to save Gonzo's for Poppy *and* learn to bowl well enough to participate in a championship? What if she said yes to Patrick and then played terribly on game day? She didn't want to let down her friends. She'd never had friends count on her like this. Then again, even if her game was off, any little bit she could help the team score would be better than forfeiting all together, right?

"Who's Mr. Martin?" Zoey asked, hoping to buy herself more time before she had to make her decision.

"This old guy who used to own another bowling center, and left a chunk of money in his will to keep the Summer League going," Patrick explained. "He actually founded it a million years ago for his own kids to have something to do in the summer."

"The championship used to be held at his bowling center," Tyler jumped in. "That's where we practiced last summer. It was next to the mall. But he died and his family sold the land, and the bowling center's being torn down to make condos."

"Oh, and did we mention the cash prize?" Isa asked excitedly.

Zoey's ears perked up.

"Cash prize?"

"Mr. Martin left a cash prize for the winner of the tournament—two thousand dollars! If we win, the five of us will split the prize evenly. We think Patrick should still get his share because he's our captain and is coaching us," Lacey said.

Hope ballooned in Zoey's chest, edging out the nerves. She knew that four hundred dollars wasn't enough to pay off Poppy's mortgage and stave off Mr. Silos, but hey, it couldn't hurt.

"Okay, I'm in so long as everyone keeps their expectations super low," Zoey said, smiling shyly. "And try to feel better soon, Patrick."

"We're going to teach you everything we know," he promised, rubbing the splint on his finger.

"I'll do my best," Zoey promised. "But, uh, can we chill a little? I mean, this is just bowling, right?"

She laughed nervously. But Patrick's gaze remained blank and humorless.

"This is serious, Zoey," he said, staring at her intensely

as if they were about to face the apocalypse and Zoey alone could ensure the survival of the human race.

"Oh yeah, I mean, I know," Zoey said, trying to match his somber tone. The butterflies in her stomach morphed into dinosaurs. And then those dinosaurs unearthed a soccer ball and turned Zoey's entire digestive tract into their own personal stadium. "I'm, ah, just going to go grab my lucky bowling ball."

"Hey, Zoey?" Tyler said, following her. He handed her the multicolored ball he knew she liked from the biggest rack in the corner of the alley. The ball was blue with swirls of green, brown, and white, and reminded Zoey of a globe designed to look like abstract art. She'd nicknamed it her Earth Ball, and loved how holding it and heaving its heft down the lane made her feel powerful. Like she not only had the whole world in her hands, but could send it whizzing off to do her bidding whenever she wanted. Now she just had to figure out how to make it roll strikes.

"Yeah?"

Tyler turned to face Zoey, his face as solemn as Patrick's. "I'm going to need you to bowl like your life depends on it."

Zoey clutched her Earth Ball tighter. "Yeah, I know how hard you guys have been practicing, and I'll definitely do my best."

"Your best?" Tyler mocked, tapping his foot petulantly. "Sorry, but I'm going to need more than your best. I'm going to need you to sign this contract, agreeing to cut off your own right arm in the event you fail to win us the Summer Big Bowl Championship."

It took a moment for Zoey to realize he was kidding. She burst out laughing, and Tyler joined in.

"Don't let Patrick psych you out," Tyler said, choosing a sleek black ball from the rack in front of them. "And, I mean, bowling's great and everything, but duuude, it's just a game."

"I'm scared of messing up," Zoey confessed.

"Don't worry about it. I lost us the championship last summer," Tyler whispered. "It only took six months for Patrick to talk to me again."

Zoey froze. "Seriously?"

"Kidding!" Tyler reassured her. "It was more like six minutes. He just had to scrape himself off the floor after fainting."

"Haha," said Zoey.

"Fine, he didn't really faint. But I did really lose us the tournament."

"What happened?" Zoey asked, wondering if she truly wanted to know, or whether the story would just make her more nervous.

"I don't know. I think Isa might, with all her math formulas," Tyler said honestly. "But all I know is I tried my hardest. I thought I was about to get a strike, but I only got nine pins. The other team bowled a strike. Eric got the strike, actually. I think that's why Patrick acted like such an idiot in front of him yesterday."

"Oh," Zoey said. "That's it?"

"Yup," said Tyler, so good-naturedly that Zoey couldn't help feeling better. "And Patrick survived. Plus, everyone knows you're new. Even Patrick. Even if he's all cranky and acting like you owe him your soul and future unborn children. So don't worry. Seriously, everything is going to be okay. We're all just grateful you agreed to fill in."

Zoey was so touched it took her a while to find the right words. "Thanks. Thanks for the pep talk."

"Any time," said Tyler, with a friendly wink.

From the corner of her eye, Zoey spotted Lacey hovering a few steps to their right, chewing the inside of her cheek and watching Zoey and Tyler talk. Remembering Lacey's crush, Zoey subtly stepped back so Lacey would have room to step up and join the chat.

"But, you know, I'm going to need a lot more than pep talks. I need more tips from the pros. Lacey, you're so good at getting spares. What's your secret? I feel like I lose momentum after my first roll."

Nervously twisting her hair tie around her wrist, Lacey launched into an explanation of her strategy that seemed to impress even Tyler. Something about the arrows and scuff marks on the floor of the lane. Zoey only partially understood, but she could tell Lacey and Tyler were getting along better than they had all week and that made her happy.

The team practiced for a solid three hours. Soon Zoey's head spun with bowling advice—from Isa's geometry to Patrick's superstitions. But it was Lacey's tips that seemed to become less logical the longer they practiced.

"Remember to match your accessories to your bowling ball on game day," she advised Zoey sagely.

Isa laughed. Patrick groaned, and Tyler rolled his eyes.

"Hey! Don't knock it till you've tried it," Lacey said defensively, adjusting the purple bangles stacked on her left wrist, which paired nicely with her lavender bowling ball. "When I wear a power outfit, I feel more confident. And when I feel confident, I bowl better."

Zoey glanced up at the screen. "Lacey's score is three points higher than yours today, Ty. Maybe we should get you a few red bracelets," she teased. Tyler had switched halfway through practice to a heavier red ball. His cheeks pinked, but to Zoey's surprise, he took her suggestion seriously.

"I guess it can't hurt to try," he mumbled.

"I'm so glad to hear you say that," Lacey said, whipping a few burgundy bands from her monogrammed canvas tote. She handed them to Tyler, who eyed the bracelets skeptically at first, then shrugged and slipped them on.

"You brought a bunch of jewelry to a bowling alley?" he asked.

"I prefer to think of it as I came prepared to practice." Lacey smiled. Tyler smiled back, amused. No one noticed Zoey smiling the biggest of all, watching them.

The team played for another three hours before Zoey spotted Toni-Ann heading briskly to the exit. Zoey hadn't even realized she was there.

"I'll be right back," Zoey told Patrick, and ran after Toni-Ann.

"Toni-Ann! Hi! Did you come to see José? He's at the dentist, but he'll be back soon. Maybe you could talk to Poppy now?"

Toni-Ann frowned. "I just talked to him. Sorry, Zoey. Your Poppy said he doesn't want the Triple Threat Chicken Café to supply food to the arcade."

"What? *Why?*"

"He didn't say why. Only that he appreciated the

offer, but it wasn't necessary because the arcade has its own kitchen on site."

"But that doesn't make any sense!" Zoey exclaimed, swallowing down the lump that had suddenly formed at the back of her throat. "What is Poppy thinking? Everything in that kitchen is broken. We can't use it to cook lunch for customers."

Toni-Ann gave Zoey a sympathetic smile. "I don't know. And I'm sorry it didn't work out. I know you were really hoping for a partnership. But I gotta run. My shift starts in ten minutes. Let José know I stopped by, okay?"

Zoey nodded, frustrated, and watched Toni-Ann walk out the door with yet another of Zoey's plans for saving Gonzo's that Poppy had rejected.

What was wrong with her grandfather?

Angry, Zoey ran to the broom closet he used as an office at the back of the bowling alley.

"Poppy! We have to talk!"

Poppy sat at his desk and glanced up from the computer at Zoey. His reading glasses slid down his nose.

"*¿Qué pasa mija?*"

"I think you're making a big mistake saying no to Toni-Ann. We might be able to get a lot more customers if we offer them lunch, and the Triple Threat Chicken Café's sandwiches are legendary on the boardwalk."

Poppy sighed heavily.

"I had a feeling you sent her to talk to me." He shook his head sadly and went back to typing. "I thought we talk about this the other night when you try to clean the lanes with hand soap, eh? I want you to relax, my little *jefa*, to enjoy being a kid. But you are so much like your mami. Always wanting to help."

"Then let me help!" Zoey said.

"Zoey, we cannot just change everything now. Don't you remember how Abuela used to make the menu every week? The restaurant side of the business was her dream, and she cooked food so delicious. We were the only bowling alley in Jersey that sell *frijoles negros* and *plátanitos fritos*." His eyes warmed with the memory, then misted. He took off his glasses and wiped them on his shirt hem.

"I always hope your mami would move back and take over the café," Poppy said. "And then one summer when you visited, I can tell she seriously consider the offer for the first time. Your father just had something else fall through and she needed the work. But she want to bring new foods here, from culinary school and being on the road. She no respect the past and Abuela's vision." He glanced down at a framed picture on his desk of Abuela and a nine-year-old Mami. Zoey's mom and grandma wore matching chef hats in the fading photo, and beamed at the camera. A huge tray of *picadillo* and green olives they must have cooked together sat in front of them.

"You don't know how lucky you and José are to be born here and to grow up speaking the language. All you need to do to succeed is work hard. You can grow up to do whatever you want," he said, digressing.

"I know we're lucky. And I'm sorry Mami didn't want to cook with Abuela, but what does any of that have to do with partnering with Toni-Ann?" Zoey asked, growing impatient.

But it was as if Poppy hadn't heard Zoey. He continued, "It broke my heart when your mami, she leave me and your abuela all alone here with the business we built our whole life for *her*. Sometimes I wonder what is the point to all this. Why fight for something that's already been lost?" He stared sadly down at his computer.

Zoey's anger faded like the old photo on Poppy's desk. She'd always thought the past few years were hard for her and José, moving all over the country with Dad after Mami died. But now, for the first time, Zoey wondered what Poppy's days had been like, alone in the home and the business he'd once shared with his wife and daughter. Suddenly, Zoey felt like bursting into tears. She wanted to crawl into Poppy's lap like a little kid and let them both dissolve into gray mist. But that would be wallowing. And her mami and abuela weren't wallowers. They had been dream weavers—the kind of people who overcame challenges and worked hard so they could stitch together the life they wanted to live. They wouldn't have let Poppy or Zoey get swept away by sadness.

"Mami was a happy person," Zoey said gently. "Like, I know you don't think so, but she was really happy with Dad, and she *liked* moving all the time. She'd make moving into an adventure. Even José liked moving around when she was alive. We moved less then, too. Only once a year or every two years, and always in the summer so that we would have already finished school. She made us feel like we were special because we got to see new places. She'd tell us, 'Everyone else is staying in their boring suburbs, but the Finolios are off to see the world!'"

"Yeah?" Poppy asked, sounding doubtful.

"Yeah," repeated Zoey, but more firmly. "And she'd take us on field trips and teach us about the places we lived. Like, we went to the Grand Canyon when we moved to Arizona, then to Mount Rushmore when we moved to South Dakota. We sat in a ton of live studio audiences for TV screenings in LA the year Dad's dream was to be an actor, and he was an extra in a bunch of sitcoms. It was super cool! And Mami and Dad never fought. Not like other kids' parents. They were so in love. Dad used to make breakfast for Mami every morning. Scrambled eggs and a caramel cappuccino from this fancy espresso machine that moved to every new place with us. She used to say she'd start her day anywhere if she could start it with a cup of his coffee. That they should open a coffee shop. But he never wanted to. He said his coffee was just for her, and she'd smile and kiss him and tell him he was a romantic. It was actually a little gross." Zoey wrinkled her nose, remembering her parents' constant PDA.

Poppy glanced up in surprise.

"I guess I never saw that side of their relationship," he said slowly. "I just thought Michael was keeping Jasmeen away from her home and her parents and our family business, running away whenever life got hard. But if your mami was really happy . . ." He trailed off, looking at Zoey questioningly.

"I think she was," Zoey whispered, meaning it and wishing Mami was still alive to back her up. "And, Poppy, she didn't forget you. She told us stories about growing up with you and Abuela. And sometimes she even put Cuban twists on the food when she made us dinner at home."

Poppy tossed his glasses on his desk and put his hands up to his eyes, covering them. His shoulders shook and Zoey realized that he was crying. Swallowing hard she bravely continued, "I think she built her dream on top of yours, like a house on a foundation or the sequel to a novel. She didn't want to just relive your story with Abuela, but to write new chapters with all of us."

It was quiet for a long time, but when Poppy finally looked at her his eyes were shiny and looked smaller without the glasses' magnifying effect. They reminded Zoey of the beads on a big eighties necklace she'd found in Mami's dresser—dark brown sequins that had dulled over the years.

"Thank you for sharing this with me. And I'm sorry, *mija*. For the terrible thing I say to your dad before he leave. I know he not responsible for your mami dying. The doctors said she had an undetected birth defect. I raised her, and even I didn't know," Poppy said heavily. He shook his head. "Anyway, I'm going to try to get along better with Michael. For you and José. And for Jasmeen. I know she always wish I could be more accepting. And if you say she was happy with your dad, then that's all that matters."

Poppy paused to wipe at the corners of his eyes with his hand. "I just wish I could talk to your mami one more time," he confided.

"Me too," Zoey said in a small voice. "But sometimes I think I know what she would say even though she isn't here to say it herself."

"Oh yeah?"

"Yeah. I think Mami would say maybe you're the one running away now, Poppy," Zoey said slowly. Her thoughts were a jumble, but a couple kept rising to the top of the pile: How Isa had been right about Zoey needing to work things out with Lacey instead of leaving the sleepover early. How the Curve Breakers refused to quit even when their captain and most dedicated member was hurt.

"It's like you're running away while standing still. You're giving up on your dream by not letting me or Toni-Ann or anyone else help you try to save the bowling alley. Okay, you're not moving to another state like Dad the second a job doesn't work out, but you're also not fighting for what you want. I bet Mami and Abuela would have wanted you to fight for Gonzo's. Shouldn't you take your own advice that you gave Dad and really commit to your one big dream?"

Poppy's eyes widened in surprise. He gazed tenderly down at Zoey.

"*Ay*, my sweet granddaughter, you are so smart. Just like your mami. And you're right. Of course, you're right.

The worst task *es la que no se hace*, eh? The one you don't do," he said. Zoey smiled—that had been another one of Mami's favorite sayings.

"I should go talk to Toni-Ann and see if she still wants to sell those amazing chicken avocado sandwiches here," Poppy said, standing and closing his laptop with a decisive click.

Zoey held her breath. Had she actually gotten through to Poppy? She watched him hopefully, not daring to speak.

"Thank you, *mija*," he called over his shoulder as he walked out.

Zoey felt more inspired than she had in a long time. And then another idea popped into her head as she rejoined her teammates, still practicing under Patrick's determined watch.

"Hey, guys, what if we hold the Summer Big Bowl Championship here at Gonzo's? Poppy could sure use the business."

No one answered at first. Everyone looked over at Patrick, who pensively bent down to pull the championship rules up on his phone.

"We're not in charge of the location. All the teams have to agree on one, according to Mr. Martin's Summer League rules, and we already did," he said finally, sounding sorry. "Oh man. I almost forgot. It's going to be at that place where Eric and his team practice."

"Oh," Zoey said.

"But maybe we could try to convince the other teams to agree to a change in venue?" asked Isa hopefully. "Like if Gonzo's can sweeten the deal somehow? Maybe offer a bigger discount on the entrance fee?"

"Yeah?" Zoey turned back to Patrick. "We could definitely offer a bigger discount."

"Maybe if we gave this place a makeover, like, super fast," Lacey said, eyeing the peeling paint and scuffed lanes.

"Definitely! We could clean Gonzo's up and finish fixing everything and advertise the championship as Gonzo's Grand Comeback! We could make this a really big event! Oh my gosh, this could actually maybe save my grandfather's bowling alley," Zoey said, half talking to herself, half trying to convince the group.

"I'm in! Let's do it. Let's try to convince the other teams!" Isa said, smiling. "I mean, Zoey's helping us out at the last minute. She's doing us a huge favor by filling in. We can try to help Gonzo's. And, for real, all our best practices have been here."

"I'm in too," Tyler said.

"Okay, I'll start calling the other team captains after practice today," Patrick agreed.

"I'll help," Lacey offered.

Zoey's insides dissolved into a puddle of rainbows and heart emojis and friendship bracelets. The next few days were going to be capital-B Busy, and she couldn't wait.

10

atrick and Lacey talked to everyone they knew—building up buzz for Gonzo's Grand Comeback and trying to persuade the other teams to move the Summer Big Bowl Championship. Within two days, they got the green light. A few of the other bowlers' parents even fondly remembered bowling at Gonzo's when they were kids themselves. They hadn't realized Gonzo's was still around. Poppy gave his blessing as well, and the gang got to work on the old building's makeover.

No one had better redecorating ideas or access to cooler stuff than Lacey. A few months earlier her parents had hosted an outer-space-themed gala for the PTA, and there were laser lights, silvery moon decals, gold tablecloths, and more supplies just sitting in her basement, waiting to be put to use again. With Poppy's permission, Zoey and her friends painted the walls of the arcade an ombre black that faded to gray, then pinned twinkling holiday lights from the ceiling when the paint dried. The effect was an ethereal, almost magical glow. Patrick and Tyler helped José finish fixing most of the game machines. The motorcycle game, though, stubbornly refused all medical attention.

José was working on it a few days later when he called out, "Zo! Come here! Maybe you can get this screw out. Your hands are smaller than ours. It's stuck."

Zoey ran over to the machine where Patrick, Tyler, and José sat frowning. The motorcycle you were supposed to sit on while virtually racing in the video game reminded her of Dad. He still hadn't called or responded to any of her texts or voice mails. She'd lost track of how many she'd left him. Trying not to think about it, Zoey sat down to help José.

"Here," he said, showing her where the screw had jammed. She slipped her fingers into the compartment, but the screw wouldn't budge.

"Forget it, this one's a waste of time," José said, standing and wiping his forehead. "I'm going to talk to Poppy. I think maybe we should just move it to the back. Tyler, why don't you and Zoey go clean the lanes? Use the special cleaning equipment Poppy left in lane ten."

He turned to Zoey. "Don't use hand soap again. Poppy was pretty, ah, upset about it."

She nodded.

"Patrick, let's go install the laser lights at the entrance."

"Okay," Patrick said. "But then the team has to squeeze in another hour of practice."

"Nooo. I'm good," Tyler said, yawning. "I think I've peaked."

"Maybe. But if you have, the extra practice won't hurt. If you haven't, then we can improve your performance. I don't want a repeat of last year. We have to maximize your potential, Tyler," Patrick said before heading with an extremely amused José to Poppy's cramped office to pick up the laser lights that Poppy kept muttering were a tripping hazard. Tyler and Zoey walked over to the scuffed lanes.

"Tell you a secret?" Tyler asked.

"Sure," Zoey said, wondering if he was about to confide a secret crush on somebody. If so, she hoped it was on Lacey since she already liked him.

"I'm excited for this championship, but I'm trying out for the baseball team too this year at school," he said quietly.

"Oh, that's great, Tyler!"

"Don't tell Patrick though," Tyler warned.

Zoey laughed. "There's no way I'm telling Patrick. You can break his heart all on your own."

Tyler's shoulders slumped. "I'm not trying to hurt his feelings! That's part of the problem. He takes bowling so personally. Like, dude, just because you want to go pro doesn't mean we all do. For some of us, this is just supposed to be a fun hobby. And he's extra hard on me because my mom's a professional bowler. He expects me to, like, breathe bowling twenty-four seven. But I want to try other stuff too. High school's not that far away. I have to start thinking ahead. If I do baseball, maybe I'll be able to make the JV team in high school, you know?"

"I hear you," Zoey said. "And I didn't know your mom was a professional bowler. That's so cool!"

Tyler smiled. "Yeah, but I swear she puts less pressure on me than Patrick!"

Zoey laughed, and they got to work oiling the lanes.

"How is it so *easy* for you to talk to guys?" Lacey asked Zoey later, as they stood on ladders pasting glow-in-the-dark stars to the bowling alley's ceiling.

"I don't know," Zoey said. "Maybe because the people closest to me are all guys. José, Dad, Poppy. Especially José. Moving around so much, I haven't had a chance to learn all of the girly stuff you and Isa are into."

"Yeah, that makes sense," said Lacey dully. "I just wish I knew how to get Tyler to notice me. Like, we have nothing to talk about if it's not about bowling. I turn into, like, a mouse if I'm alone with him. I get so tongue-tied. It's pathetic."

Zoey shrugged. "So, just don't think about it."

"What do you mean?"

"I mean, pretend you don't have a crush so you can just be yourself without getting nervous. You have tons of personality. And you're definitely no mouse."

Lacey laughed at that. "What do you talk about with Tyler and other guys?" she asked.

"Sports, mostly," said Zoey, adding splashes of iridescent glittery paint to the spaces between the stars she'd stuck to the ceiling, and passing the paintbrush to Lacey to do the same.

"Sometimes we talk about books or movies. Music. Video games. Videos or memes that have gone viral online. With José, I talk about anything. But that's different because he's my brother. Sports are usually a safe bet, though, with a lot of guys. Do you like any sports besides bowling?"

Lacey thought about it. "Not really. Well actually, my dad got season tickets to the Yankees, so I started going to games with him this summer."

"Awesome!" Zoey couldn't even tell Lacey how perfect it was that she'd recently discovered an interest in baseball, for fear Lacey would spill Tyler's secret to Patrick about trying out for the baseball team. "You should try talking to Tyler about baseball."

"Are you sure? I don't really know that much yet."

"I'm sure. Aren't you the one who told me I'm good at talking to guys?" Zoey shrugged.

"Yeah."

"So listen to me," Zoey said confidently.

"Haha. Okay," Lacey said, handing the paintbrush back to Zoey to add more glitter to her part of the ceiling.

"I have a question for you, too."

"What?"

Zoey hesitated. She wanted to ask Lacey for style tips, but Lacey could be so blunt with her opinions. What if she told Zoey she thought she was too ugly and a lost cause? Or what if Lacey didn't insult Zoey's looks, but urged her to buy a bunch of expensive clothes and accessories that she couldn't afford? Then Zoey would feel doubly insecure about her both lacking fashion sense and lacking budget.

Then again, Zoey thought about how Lacey had trusted her enough to share her crush on Tyler. Maybe they were becoming real friends. And this wasn't exactly the type of thing that Zoey could talk about with José or Poppy or Dad. Heck, she couldn't even get ahold of Dad!

"How do you do the whole girly thing?"

"What is this 'girly thing' you speak of?" Lacey said, laughing. "Girls can do anything guys can do, and vice versa."

Zoey took a deep breath, trying to find the right words to explain.

"I mean, like, I want to wear makeup and dress better, but I don't really know what'll look okay on me, you know? All I have are jeans and José's old T-shirts. I don't know how to do my hair or put on much makeup. Sometimes I just feel really ugly."

"What? You're definitely not ugly, and you're being way too hard on yourself. Stop worrying about what other people think—just be you," Lacey said. She then artfully pasted a few stars to the top of the wall so it looked like they were raining down from the ceiling.

"I know, but . . . I was wondering if maybe you could show me anyway?" Zoey asked quietly.

Lacey froze and stared at Zoey. "You want me to give you a makeover?!" she squealed.

They hadn't so much as clicked through looks online yet, and the excited gleam in Lacey's eyes already overwhelmed Zoey.

"I—" Zoey began.

Lacey let out an exaggerated gasp, cutting her off.

"We can go shopping this afternoon! Hang on, I'll see if my dad or sister can give us a ride to the mall." Lacey whipped her phone out of the pocket of her trendy denim romper.

"Wait! No! I can't go to the mall today," Zoey said quickly. "I, uh, I can't really afford to buy any new clothes. I was just hoping maybe you could give me some tips on working with what I've got."

Lacey stopped texting.

"No problem! Let's go to my house later instead! I've got bags of old clothes I was going to donate. I can give them to you instead! You can keep whatever fits."

Zoey cringed. "I'm not your charity case, Lacey!"

Lacey flashed Zoey her signature "you must have come from Mars" look. "Don't be like that. We're friends! Isa and I borrow each other's clothes all the time." Lacey held out her wrist and shook it. "This bracelet is Isa's."

"But I don't have anything to lend you in return," Zoey pouted.

"Actually you do," Lacey said, twirling the elephant charms on the bangle she'd borrowed from Isa. "You were wearing a Yankees jersey the other day. Can I borrow that to go to the game with my dad?"

"Don't you prefer to just buy your own?" Zoey asked.

"I was going to, but yours has adorbs cut-outs on the

sleeves and that crisscross lacing in the back. I couldn't find anything that cool online. Where'd you get it?"

Zoey burst out laughing.

"A pen broke in my backpack and leaked red ink all over. I couldn't get the stains out, so I cut up the jersey so it wouldn't look gross."

"No way! You're, like, a super talented fashion designer!"

Zoey blushed.

"That's, like, the only thing I've ever sewed in my life."

Lacey continued staring at Zoey in awe.

"You should try sewing more stuff then."

"Maybe," Zoey said casually, starting to get excited. "But I have to help save Gonzo's for Poppy first. And help you guys win the championship."

Leaning on her ladder, Lacey put down the star she was about to glue to the ceiling and looked at Zoey appraisingly, reminding Zoey of how Isa had studied her the same way in the bathroom on the day they'd first met. Thoughtful, but not judging her.

"You're such a nice person, it's borderline annoying," Lacey said finally.

"Huh?"

"You're like Harry Potter with the savior complex. You're always trying to help everyone. Your grandpa with

Gonzo's. Our team with bowling. Me with Tyler. Whatever. I know I shouldn't get annoyed with you for being kind—being a good person is what matters most. Blah blah blah."

"If being a good person matters so much, then why do so many people make such a big deal about how they look all the time?" Zoey said, raising an eyebrow.

"I don't know—the world does seem to have it backward, don't they?" Lacey admitted, twirling her ponytail pensively around her finger. After a brief pause she continued, "But I think you can be both—well dressed *and* a good person. My mom always says, 'You see the frosting before you bite into the cake, so you may as well add sprinkles.'"

"What's *that* supposed to mean?"

"That what's inside is most important, but what you put on the outside sends a message too, so why not have fun with your style and figure out what clothes help you feel the most confident? That's what I was saying the other day about picking a power outfit to wear on championship day," Lacey said, adding more glitter to her side of the ceiling.

"Anyway," Lacey continued, "I'm happy to help with a full makeover or just with picking out a power outfit. Let me know whenever you're ready."

"Thanks," Zoey said.

Zoey went back to painting and quietly mulled over Lacey's words, trying to ignore the little voice at the back of her mind that worried no outfit would ever look good enough to give her the kind of confidence she needed. But then, if what Lacey said was true, perhaps she didn't need new clothes at all. Maybe she should just focus on trying to be confident without thinking at all about what she was wearing.

Hmmm. Zoey stuck another star on the ceiling and decided she didn't have to make any decisions about it right now. She had enough on her plate already, what with practicing for the upcoming championship and helping Poppy. Once the championship was behind her and Gonzo's was safe, then she'd revisit her feelings on fashion.

That afternoon, Isa invited Zoey over to her house to make flyers advertising the bowling championship and to spread the word online. Zoey braced herself to be intimidated by another mansion, but to her surprise, Isa's narrow, two-story house looked almost exactly like Poppy's—from the crisp gray exterior to the peeling white deck—and was only a few blocks away. She lived on the other side of the boardwalk, closer to the Triple Threat Chicken Café, with her parents, grandparents, and little twin siblings.

The inside of Isa's house was chaos. Toddlers tossed Cheerios at each other from their matching high chairs. Her abuelo shouted at a Mets game on TV. Isa's mom drank coffee from an enormous microwave-safe mug in one hand and toweled peanut butter out of the twins' hair with the other. Stuffed animals, building blocks, and other toys covered nearly every inch of the floor. Nineties ballads blasted from an FM radio sitting atop the refrigerator.

"Hi, sweetie! Nice to meet you, Zoey," Mrs. Levine called cheerily when the girls walked in the door. "We have some *pastelitos de guayaba* if you're hungry."

Zoey's ears perked up. The widespread availability of *pastelitos* in Miami had been one of her favorite things about living there. Before that, she hadn't eaten one of those delicious, flaky-dough pastries since before Mami passed away.

"Any other flavors besides *guayaba*?" Isa asked, frowning at the brown paper bag from the Cuban bakery sitting on the kitchen counter.

"I think some might have cheese only. The majority are *guayaba* and cheese though."

"That sounds so yummy. My mom used to make pastelitos with guava and cheese," Zoey said, her mouth watering.

"Then please, help yourself." Mrs. Levine waved in the general direction of the kitchen, finished cleaning the twins' hair, and popped fruit pouches in their mouths. She closed her eyes, wrapped both hands around her coffee cup, and took a long sip. In that second, one of the twins squirted his fruit pouch clear across the room, coating a lamp, the coffee table, and even Abuelo's bald head in applesauce. Mrs. Levine sighed, drained her coffee, and balanced the cup on top of all the other dishes already waiting to be washed in the sink.

"You might want to take the *pastelitos* upstairs to Isa's room where it's a little more quiet," she told the girls, grabbing paper towels to clean up the mess.

The stairs creaked as Isa and Zoey climbed. And Zoey nearly fell back down them when she spotted Isa's grandma on the landing. For a second, Zoey thought she was seeing her own abuela, somehow back from the dead. Isa's grandmother had the same hair-sprayed helmet of gray hair, gold-rimmed glasses, bright red jeans, and flowery, button-down blouse that Poppy's late wife used to wear. The two must have shopped at the same stores and visited the same hairdresser.

"*¡Ay!* Good, Isa, you're home," her abuela said, clapping her hands together. "And who is your friend? I don't think I meet her before? *Hola, linda.* You can call me

Abuela Graciela, like Isa." Abuela Graciela leaned in to give Zoey a quick peck on the cheek.

"Hi, I'm Zoey," she said. "I'm on the bowling team with Isa."

Up close, Zoey realized the resemblance between Abuela Graciela and her own grandmother was less pronounced than she'd originally thought in the dim light of the staircase. Abuela Graciela's eyes were brown instead of blue. Her nose was smaller, and she had more wrinkles. Also, the flowers on her shirt were teensy yellow tulips. Zoey's abuela's flowered shirt had been patterned in pink rosebuds.

"*¡Ven conmigo!* I bought you *azabaches* for the whole team today," Abuela Graciela said, pulling Isa into a hug.

"Why do we need *azabaches* for a bowling tournament?" Isa asked.

"For protection and good luck," Abuela Graciela answered, as though it were obvious. She let Isa go and beckoned for the girls to follow her into the bedroom. She retrieved a beige purse big enough to fit a box of cereal. Abuela Graciela rummaged through her purse, pulling out her wallet, wads of crumpled-up tissues, and ten packets of Splenda before she finally found what she was looking for.

"Aha!" she said, brandishing a small, white cardboard box as a toy poodle came running down the hall and nipped at Zoey's ankles. Zoey squealed, wondering if Poppy was the only person in New Jersey who did not own a loud little dog.

"He don't bite. That's Herman," Abuela Graciela told Zoey, rolling her R and pronouncing the dog's name *errrr-man*. Isa picked Herman up and gave him a snuggle.

"Okay, *ya, los encontré*. I find my *azabaches* now," Abuela Graciela said, opening the door across the hall. "Let's go to Isa's room and I'll give them to you."

Zoey gasped. The walls in Isa's room were light blue, and a painting of a tree reminiscent of a bedroom movie set grew out of the corner opposite a bed overflowing with pastel cushions. Tiny floating shelves dotted the painted tree with three-dimensional ivory flowers and doves, as well as stacks of books and a teddy bear. Clouds floated across the ceiling, which was painted light blue too. A silhouette of the New York skyline tattooed the wide white dresser, which was topped with a luggage-size makeup case. In short, Isa's room was as cool as its resident. Zoey glanced around enviously, wishing both that she could live somewhere long enough to decorate and that she could be as creative in her decor ideas as Isa.

Abuela Graciela pulled out two black onyx charms dangling from safety pins from her cardboard jewelry box. She handed one to Isa and one to Zoey.

"Wow! I haven't seen one of these in so long! My mom and grandmother were Cuban too. They used to wear them," Zoey said, gently stroking the *azabache* bead.

Isa tossed hers on the nightstand and rolled her eyes. "Abuela! This is silly. There's no math or science to wearing an *azabache* for luck."

"Shh," Abuela Graciela said, as if she didn't want the *azabaches* to hear and change their mind about helping Isa and her friends. "Didn't Patrick break his finger after he saw that boy from the other team?"

"Yes," Isa said, more impatiently than Zoey had ever heard her. "But that was because he was being dumb and showing off."

"*Sí, sí,* of course showing off is bad, but *también* the *mal de ojo* is everywhere. A little protection can't hurt. Listen to your grandma. I have experience," she said, nodding wisely.

Isa rolled her eyes again, but her grandmother just turned to Zoey.

"Promise me you'll give these to the rest of the team and make my stubborn *nieta* wear hers?" She handed Zoey the cardboard jewelry box with the rest of the charms.

"Oh, um, sure. Thank you!" Zoey said.

Isa's grandmother smiled.

"Perfect." She glanced up at the sun-shaped clock above Isa's window. It was 7:05 p.m. "I'll let you girls get to work," she said, bolting out of the room so quickly she knocked over Isa's desk chair.

"Is she okay?"

Isa laughed, setting the sleek purple chair back on its wheels. "Yeah, she's probably just running to go fight my grandfather over the big TV downstairs. He's my dad's dad. And she's my mom's mom. But you'd think they're an old married couple from the way they bicker, especially over the TV. She's a few minutes late for her favorite telenovela."

"Awww. I think your grandmother is the sweetest," Zoey said, missing her own abuela, who'd also taken her Spanish soap operas quite seriously and extolled the virtues of *azabaches* too.

Zoey had worn the one Abuela had given her until it broke a couple of years ago in Kansas. Dad wouldn't give her the money to replace it. He didn't believe in good luck charms any more than Isa did, but Zoey thought there was something to the good intentions with which they were given, and she was excited to have an *azabache* of her own to wear again.

"Abuela's so superstitious," Isa sighed. "Like, wearing an *azabache* won't help our game, you know? Practicing will. Figuring out the right angle to roll a strike. I wish she'd be more logical."

"I need your genius, math- and science-based bowling tips. But your grandma's good luck charm makes me happy too. Honestly, I'll take all the help I can get."

"Fiiine," Isa said. She opened the safety pin, slipped off the *azabache,* and threaded its top loop through the thin gold chain that she always wore around her neck.

Zoey didn't have a necklace anymore—her own gold chain had broken somewhere in Florida—so she pinned the *azabache* to the front of her faded anime T-shirt and grabbed a cheese and guava *pastelito* from the paper bag Isa had brought upstairs.

"I feel so Cuban right now," Zoey said happily.

Isa paused from firing up her laptop and turned toward Zoey. She raised an eyebrow. *"Solamente hoy?"* Just today? she asked in Spanish with no discernible accent.

"Más o menos. Kind of," Zoey replied shyly, aware of her thick American accent.

Isa looked at her questioningly. "What do you feel the rest of the time?"

"I don't know. Not enough of anything? My dad isn't Cuban. And he threw out or packed away all the Cuban stuff my mom had after she died. He got rid of all her things, actually. Except for the blanket she gave me, because I insisted on keeping it. It's mean of him, don't you think? Shouldn't my mom's culture be a part of me too?" Zoey asked in a small voice.

Isa's face grew serious. "Of course. And it already is, no matter what. But maybe it just hurts too much for him, being reminded of your mom. You said he got rid of *all* her stuff, not just the Cuban stuff."

Zoey hadn't thought of it that way. She wondered if that was why he'd started moving more often after Mami died. They only used to move once a year in the summer when Mami was alive; now they moved up to five times a school year. Did Dad think he could forget the pain if he moved around enough times? If he didn't have Mami's stuff around to remind him?

"Maybe," she said, softening and wishing that Dad would call or text her back soon.

11

Two days before the championship, Gonzo's sported new paint, gleaming lanes, and (almost) a fully functioning arcade. Only the Skee-Ball machine stubbornly refused to cooperate. But José said he would keep trying to fix it. The rubber at the bottom of Zoey's shoes felt extra springy as she and the team practiced. With Isa's brilliant tips and Abuela Graciela's good luck *azabache* pinned to her soccer jersey, Zoey's bowling score shot skyward. She rolled spares as regularly as Lacey and Tyler now. She might never be as good as Patrick or Isa, but who knew? Maybe if she formally made the school team next year she'd be a pro bowler like Tyler's mom someday. Or a fashion designer, Zoey thought excitedly, remembering her conversation with Lacey.

Halfway through the third game, Mr. Silos waltzed

in the door, sweating in his designer charcoal suit. Lacey and Tyler had to bowl before it'd be Zoey's turn again, so she snuck away to the shoe rental counter, seemingly to grab a water bottle from her backpack, but really to eavesdrop.

"Mr. Silos," Poppy greeted him politely.

"Mr. Gonzalez," he replied, wiping his brow with a crisp white handkerchief. "The clock is ticking, and I truly hope you've decided to reconsider our offer."

"Absolutely not," Poppy said. He pointed to the giant flyer posted over the shoe rental counter.

"Look, Mr. Silos, things are about to turn around for us. My crew has really been getting the place into shape," Poppy said, winking at Zoey. "And we're hosting the Summer Big Bowl Championship in just a couple of days. We're expecting hundreds of customers will come to support the teams. This will no doubt be our most lucrative day of the year!"

Mr. Silos grunted doubtfully, but leaned over to read the sign.

"This is a *children's* tournament," Mr. Silos said pityingly, glancing down at Zoey, then back up at Poppy. "Mr. Gonzalez, we both know where we stand." He let the words hang in the air, and Poppy's fists clenched. He looked down at the floor, gritting his teeth.

"Mr. Gonzalez," Mr. Silos said more quietly, glancing at Zoey again. "Our lawyer will be in touch after the weekend. My company's offer remains more than fair, and I truly don't want to see a family man like yourself in foreclosure."

The softness and almost genuine note of concern in Mr. Silos's tone was somehow more alarming than his bullying bark. Once he'd left, Zoey asked, "Poppy, how much longer do you have to pay off your mortgage? I thought we still had some time."

Poppy's shoulders drooped, and he leaned against the shoe rental corner.

"We have until the end of the month."

"But that's *next* week!"

"*Sí*," Poppy said. "But is okay. We have the championship in just two days. We are going to turn this around. Thanks to you, *mija*. Look around—Gonzo's hasn't looked this good in years! I don't want you to worry. Promise me, eh? Promise me that you don't worry?"

"Okay," Zoey said, even though she still couldn't help but worry.

"Here, can you go put away these shoes in the closet?" Poppy handed her a plastic bin and winked. "We are going to have so many customers, I bring a few extra pairs from storage."

"Okay." Zoey smiled, deciding to hope that Poppy was right and everything really would be okay. As long as the championship was a success, it probably would be. Right? Zoey took a deep breath, willing herself to be optimistic.

She grabbed the shoes and headed toward the supply closet. The door was slightly ajar. Zoey bumped it open with her hip and flipped on the light switch. She froze when she saw José kissing Toni-Ann, next to the mops. Zoey must have let out a surprised gasp, because Toni-Ann's eyes snapped open and she stepped back. Her cheeks turned the same magenta color as her painted nails.

"What are you doing in here?" Zoey demanded.

"Go away," José said, linking his fingers through Toni-Ann's and trying to pull her back into his arms. Toni-Ann's eyes darted between Zoey and him. Zoey could tell Toni-Ann also wanted her to leave, but was too nice to say so.

"Go away, Zoey," José said again, smiling goofily at Toni-Ann, who couldn't help slipping her arms around his neck. José rested his forehead on hers. They were the very picture of an adorable couple, but the visit from Mr. Silos had made Zoey too anxious to appreciate adorable. Poppy had mere *days* before he lost Gonzo's! And José hadn't finished fixing the Skee-Ball machine yet! And *José* was the one who always finished assignments early and nagged Zoey to do her homework. How could he suddenly act so lazy *now* when the stakes for their family were so much higher than whether Zoey turned in an essay about *Little Women* on time?

Zoey knew José was starting a new relationship and that would take up some of his attention. And she liked Toni-Ann. She did. But couldn't José save the smooching till after the day's work was done?

Plus, Toni-Ann knew how much trouble Gonzo's was in. If she really cared about José, shouldn't she help him do everything possible to help him save his family's bowling alley? Anger and fear and disappointment washed over Zoey, making her dizzy.

"I'm not going away," Zoey said, crossing her arms over her chest and digging her sneakers into the floor to maintain her balance. "I can't believe you're slacking off, José! You're not done fixing the arcade. And we need this championship to be perfect. It's the only thing that can save Gonzo's from closing next week!"

"Relax, I'll get to it this afternoon," José said.

"You're such a good grandson," Toni-Ann whispered, nuzzling his nose with her nose.

"No! You have to work on it now!" Zoey screamed.

José and Toni-Ann jumped apart and turned bewildered faces at Zoey.

"What's wrong with y—"José began, but Zoey interrupted him, still yelling.

"Play kissy-face with Toni-Ann later! Don't you care about Poppy? And Dad needs a place to work when selling motorcycles falls through!"

"Zo, calm down,"José said, reaching out to try to pull her into a hug. Zoey stepped back, and José sighed. "Of course I care, but Dad will never live here with Poppy. You know that, right? They don't get along. And there are way too many memories of Mami at the Jersey Shore for him to ever agree to live here."

No. Zoey didn't know that. For Zoey, memories of Mami were just more reasons to stay. She glared at José. "Easy for you to say. You're abandoning me in a few weeks too. You're just like Dad. You *don't* care what happens to me, or to Poppy. All you want is to start over alone!"

Tears began to roll down Zoey's cheeks and she ran out of the closet, past Poppy's office, and out the back entrance to the alley outside.

It smelled like garbage and cat pee, but Zoey still sat right down next to that stinky dumpster and cried like she hadn't cried in years. Because Mami was gone, and Dad was gone too, even though he shouldn't be. Because

Zoey suddenly had nobody she could count on. Not only was José leaving soon too, he was right about Dad. If or when their father decided to turn up, she'd have to leave Poppy and the bowling alley, regardless of whether Gonzo's survived or got turned into a five-star hotel and left her grandfather bankrupt in the process.

"Zo, what's wrong?" Lacey and Isa materialized out of nowhere. Lacey plopped right down in her expensive skinny jeans next to Zoey on that dirty sidewalk and slipped an arm around her shoulders.

"It's your turn to bowl. José said you ran out. Are you okay?" Isa asked softly, taking care to spread her knee-length tulle skirt beneath her and perching delicately on Zoey's other side.

Zoey took a deep, sniffling breath. She knew she should just say she was fine and head back inside to practice, but she couldn't.

"It's just everything, you know? Like, we really need this championship to turn things around for my grandfather. And my brother is too busy with his girl-friend to help, and he says my dad won't want to live here even if we do save the bowling alley. And I like it here. I don't want to move again," Zoey said, finally admitting for the first time that she wanted to stay here permanently.

"But your grandpa wants you to stay with him, right?" Lacey said. "So maybe your dad will let you."

"Yeah, maybe you just have to talk to him," Isa said, smiling at Zoey. "Tell him there's this bowling team that can't live without you."

Zoey tried to smile back, but the tears kept coming.

"There's another reason, too. It's not just because I made friends here, or even because this is where my mom grew up. Like, part of it is I don't think I want to live with my dad anymore," she confessed out loud, in a small voice. "He hasn't returned any of my phone calls or texts since he dropped us off with Poppy."

"Wow. He sounds like a jerk," Lacey said sympathetically.

"Don't insult him," Zoey said instantly, even though she was mad at Dad for putting his own dreams ahead of making a home for his kids. She'd always known why José got angry at Dad, but now she agreed with him. And that sucked. It had been way easier closing her eyes and making excuses for Dad once upon a time.

Isa leaned around Zoey to frown at Lacey, then dropped her head on Zoey's shoulder.

"Sorry," Lacey said. "I get it. He's still your dad, and I shouldn't call him names."

"Yeah," Zoey said, letting her head fall on top of Isa's

green headband and staring down at a smashed soda can on the ground. "Thanks."

Lacey sighed and rested her head on Zoey's other shoulder.

"You can't move. We really do need you for the bowling team. So if your dad shows up and tries to steal you away, tell him he's going to have to deal with me first," Lacey said, sounding like she meant it.

Zoey smiled, picturing a Lacey-Dad confrontation: Dad would be confused, then amused, and, by the end, probably annoyed with Lacey's demands. Zoey felt a bit of the tension drain out of her body. "I'm not that good of a bowler."

"You're good enough that I think Patrick will definitely start nagging you more than Ty about 'maximizing your potential,'" Isa said, making air quotes.

"Just tell your dad your friends really, really, really want you to stay," Lacey said, and Isa nodded in agreement. Arms linked, the girls got up and headed back inside to practice.

And, even though they hadn't actually solved any of her problems, Zoey realized how good it felt to have real friends to talk to about them. Friends who wanted to stick up for you when it felt like no one else would (even if Zoey didn't actually plan to unleash Lacey on Dad). For the first time that summer, Zoey didn't feel so alone.

12

Patrick had a follow-up appointment for his fingers that afternoon and let the team go home early. Zoey had caught José watching her during practice, but she'd busied herself chatting with one of her friends each time to avoid talking to him. Now though, she had no choice but to look her brother in the eye when he walked over to the lane where she continued practicing by herself.

"You're feeling a little better?" he asked, watching her Earth Ball hurtle down the lane and topple six pins.

"I guess," Zoey said, sidestepping José to stand in front of the ball return.

"I know this is a hard summer for you, with Dad leaving and me going to college soon," José said quietly to her back. "But we've talked about this. I'll be your brother no matter where I go. You know that, right? Like, I'm still

going to love you when I go to school and everything.
You can call me anytime."

"Yeah," Zoey said in a flat voice.

She knew what José was saying was true, but she also
knew he wasn't much of a phone person. And that even if
José really did start making the effort to call her, a quick
conversation here and there wouldn't be the same as seeing each other every day. But Zoey didn't want another
big confrontation so she kept her mouth shut. The ball
return finally spit out her favorite ball. Zoey grabbed it.
All she wanted to do was practice her form.

"Toni-Ann is worried about you too," José said, after
Zoey tried another throw and her ball rolled into the
gutter. "But she can't leave the restaurant. Will you come
with me to go see her?"

Zoey looked longingly at the refreshed set of ten pins
waiting to be knocked down at the end of the lane, but
nodded in agreement. She knew she'd overreacted with
Toni-Ann and should make amends.

The Triple Threat Café was totally empty.

"They close between lunch and dinner," José explained
in response to Zoey's questioning look. He walked past the
display of rock star chickens and knocked on the glass door.
Toni-Ann opened up and aimed a warm gaze at Zoey.

"I know how important the championship is to Gonzo's, so I thought maybe we could make bowling-themed cupcakes to sell on game day," she said. "My parents agreed we can put all the profits toward saving Gonzo's."

José and Zoey both opened their mouths to protest, but Toni-Ann held up a hand.

"Oh, don't start. It's not charity. It's business. We can't partner with Poppy to sell sandwiches if Gonzo's closes down," she said matter-of-factly over her shoulder, already leading them through the swinging double doors to the café's kitchen.

Zoey gasped. Dozens of mini chocolate bars, cookies, syrups, creams, candies, and nuts sat on a wide counter beside the industrial-size oven.

"I didn't know you had a chocolate factory back here!"

Pride sparkled in Toni-Ann's dark brown eyes. "We bake all our desserts from scratch at the café. And I was thinking we could make the cupcake tops look like bowling balls. Like we could use chocolate frosting and put three white chocolate chips upside down in the corner to look like the holes in a bowling ball, or we could cut sugar cookies into the shape of bowling pins and put those on top. But those are just some ideas. Let's go wild. Be as creative as you want to be. José said you're an amazing baker, like your mom."

"Awww," Zoey said, glancing appreciatively at José, and lighting up when she saw that Toni-Ann's table of ingredients included not only cream cheese, but also guava paste.

"Doesn't this kitchen remind you a little of La Cafetera Cubana in California?" he said, seeing where Zoey's gaze had settled.

She nodded, glancing at the enormous stainless steel appliances and commercial-size bag of flour and sugar.

"What was that?" asked Toni-Ann.

"The only Cuban restaurant our mom ever worked at," Zoey said. "The owners were this elderly couple who wouldn't let her experiment with new recipes, but they loved having kids around. So she'd bring us with her to work during the summer."

"That's where Mami taught us how to cook," José added.

"You bake too?" Toni-Ann asked, sounding surprised as she tied an apron around her waist and handed José and Zoey matching aprons emblazoned with dancing chicken cartoons reflective of the café's decor.

José flipped a wooden spoon and caught it expertly. "I learned from the best," he said, shooting a bittersweet look at Zoey. And for a moment, Zoey wasn't seeing José the tall, broad eighteen-year-old, but the shorter, skinnier

ten-year-old version who'd lifted her up to pour rainbow
sprinkles all over the butter cake they'd made with Mami
for Dad's birthday in La Cafetera Cubana's kitchen. That
was the year Zoey was four and insisted on adding glitter to everything. After Zoey had finished decorating
the cake, she'd dumped the rest of the sprinkles on poor,
unsuspecting José's head. Yelping, José had dropped her
on her butt on the floor, then rained sprinkles on top of
her as he shook them out of his hair and T-shirt. Zoey
had giggled so hard she'd almost barfed, and Mami had
laughed so hard there were tears in her eyes. Mami told
Dad the story that night right before they sang happy
birthday over the cake. Chuckling, he'd said he was going
to wish for better behaved children before he blew out
the candles.

Zoey sighed. She missed Dad as much as Mami
right now.

"I can bake lemon cake balls and ice them to look
like bowling balls," Zoey volunteered, trying not to think
about how lemon was Dad's favorite flavor.

When the sun was beginning to set, José and Zoey left
Toni-Ann's and went to meet Poppy at the arcade so
they could all walk home together. As the three of them
approached Poppy's house though, Zoey saw a man sit-

ting on the front steps, a stack of pizza boxes beside him. Her heart leaped when she realized who it was, and she sprinted ahead. The man stood as she neared and Zoey flung herself into his waiting, open arms like she was still a little kid.

"Hi, Zoey," Dad said, hugging her tightly. Zoey felt like crying—she'd missed the smell of his aftershave and how safe she felt with his arms wrapped around her.

"Missed you, Zo," Dad said into her hair. Hearing those words, Zoey stiffened and stepped out of his hug.

"I missed you too! But why didn't you answer my texts? Why didn't you tell us you were coming?" Zoey blurted. Before Dad could answer, Poppy and José came up to them.

José glared at Dad without saying hello and stepped around them into the house, letting the door slam behind him.

"It's good to see you, Michael," Poppy said, gently slapping Dad's back. "Thank you for bringing dinner." He followed José inside, leaving the door open.

"Let's go in," Dad said, picking up the pizza boxes. "We can talk more then."

Zoey closed her mouth—she'd wanted to ask Dad a bunch of questions. And she was disappointed that he hadn't apologized right away for not texting her back, but maybe she should give him the benefit of the doubt one last time. Maybe he had a good excuse for disappearing on them for so long.

Once everyone was settled at the dining room table with pizza, Zoey felt it was safe to finally ask her questions. "Dad, how's the job? Do you have your own place yet? Are you still crashing on your buddy's couch?"

"New York is amazing. I went to the Statue of Liberty, Ellis Island, and the Met," Dad said. His blue eyes twinkled, but Zoey noticed he didn't answer any of her questions. "And Times Square. Oh man, Zo, you're going to love Times Square. The whole place is electric. Lights all over. Everybody hustling and bustling . . ."

Dad talked and talked, babbling on about tourist attractions. Rowboats in Central Park and musicals on Broadway. The Empire State Building and Rockefeller Center. The more Zoey listened, the more it sounded like Dad had been on vacation without them the past few weeks. Zoey noticed José watched Dad through dull eyes, like he expected nothing more and was over it, and Zoey could feel her temper flaring too. She was beginning to wonder whether he'd even started his new job.

"You do any work while you were there, eh, Michael?" Poppy asked, coming to the same conclusion as Zoey.

Dad shot Poppy a dark look.

"Of course I did," he said, tossing his pizza crust on his plate. "Selling motorcycles was the best part." He shook his head. "Actually, no, this is the best part: I'm ready for you guys to move back in with me."

Dad beamed, opening his mouth and spreading his hands like they were on a game show and they had just won the prize behind door number three. But Zoey glanced sadly around the dining room. She'd come to love the homey familiarity of Poppy's house. She loved the borderline creepy pictures of needlepoint clowns her grandmother had made and framed in the foyer and the heavy wooden furniture that hadn't moved in decades and the vases filled with fake, dusty roses. She even loved the bowl of wax fruit, and the apple that still had her bite marks from when she'd tried to eat it as a little kid.

"When, uh, when do we have to leave?" she asked.

"Tomorrow," Dad said, like it was great news. Zoey sat up so fast her chair scraped the tile with a loud screech. The day *after* tomorrow was the Summer Big Bowl Championship!

José folded his arms over his chest. "No way. I have a girlfriend now, and I'm going to college in a few weeks anyway. I'll stay with Poppy till I have to fly back down to Florida."

Poppy nodded, and Dad sighed. "Fine. I guess Zoey

and I will take on the Big Apple together," Dad said, smiling at Zoey.

Zoey couldn't smile back.

"Dad, I, uh, I'm filling in for a player who got hurt on a bowling team. And the championship is in two days at Poppy's bowling alley. It's pretty important to me. Can I please stay with Poppy till at least the championship?"

"Sorry, kiddo. But no. I have to get back to work by tomorrow," Dad said, not looking all that sorry in Zoey's opinion. She'd just told him the tournament was important to her, and he hadn't even paused to think about it before shooting her down! Zoey's hands balled into fists under the table.

Oblivious to Zoey's silent seething, Dad grabbed another slice of mushroom pizza and focused his attention on José. "New girlfriend, huh? Tell me about her."

The conversation turned to Toni-Ann, with José saying as little as possible while Dad tried asking the same questions a dozen different ways.

"She's a nice girl, Michael," Poppy finally interjected. "I know her family a long, long time. *Son buena gente.*"

Dad nodded, but he wasn't ready to get off the interrogation treadmill yet.

"What's your girlfriend like?" He tried again with José, who rolled his eyes.

"If you'd stuck around, you would have met her."

"You know that I would have if I could," said Dad slowly. José rolled his eyes again. He obviously didn't believe Dad. Neither did Zoey. Not anymore.

"Then stick around now and find out for yourself."

"You know that I can't," Dad said, a note of warning in his voice. "We have to leave first thing in the morning."

"I'll get some boxes from the basement," said Poppy.

"I'll help carry them," José said.

Zoey glared at him, then at Poppy, and finally at Dad. None of them noticed. None of them had bothered asking her what *she* wanted to do. Everyone just assumed she was leaving with Dad. Fuming inside, Zoey excused herself from the table and ran upstairs.

Alone in Mami's old room, Zoey tried texting and calling her friends to deliver the awful news about moving away, but she couldn't get phone service. For a second she thought Dad forgot to pay their bill and got even angrier at him, but then she realized it was raining outside. She knew from previous visits that sometimes cell service was bad around here during a storm. Lightning flashed, shining a brief light on the tree thrashing against Zoey's window. The way those branches shook in the wind reminded Zoey of marionettes forced into tortured choreography. Which, come to think of it, wasn't that far from how Zoey herself felt: a puppet to be yanked around and moved at her father's will. Never allowed to challenge Dad or express her own feelings for fear of hurting his. Thunder boomed outside, sounding like the rumble of a thousand bowling strikes, but louder and more satisfying. *Good*, Zoey thought. The sudden, building storm matched her mood perfectly.

"Need help packing?" José appeared in her doorway.

"No. I'm used to packing," Zoey snapped, shoving socks into every crevice of her already full backpack. "I know what to do."

José looked at her sadly, but didn't say anything. He held up his phone. "No bars. You?"

"Same."

"Okay. Guess we can look up the forecast the old-fashioned way," José said, turning on the TV beside Zoey's half-empty dresser and tuning in to the local news with the rabbit ear antennas. A grim weatherman pointed to a mass of red and yellow swirling on the radar behind him, blanketing the Jersey Shore. José whistled.

"Wow. Looks like it's going to be raining for a while."

Zoey shrugged. Moody weather was fine by her.

"Wish I could get through to Toni-Ann and just make sure she's okay though. I know her parents were going to try to keep the restaurant open as long as they could tonight." José bit his lip. Concern creased his forehead.

Zoey softened, seeing her brother's worried expression. "Why don't you use Poppy's landline to call Triple Threat Chicken's landline?"

José whipped his head up.

"Landlines. I knew the Dinosaur Age was good for something," he said, heading downstairs to use the phone mounted on the kitchen wall.

A few minutes later José popped back into Zoey's room, looking relieved.

"Thanks for the idea. They were fine. Toni-Ann got stuck at the restaurant with her parents, and they're just going to ride out the storm there."

"So I noticed you finally called her your girlfriend downstairs at dinner," Zoey teased.

"Yeah," José said, massaging the back of his neck shyly.

"What college is she going to next year?"

"University of Pennsylvania. She got into their business school. She's so smart," José said, kind of dreamily. "And she's still going to come home some weekends to help her parents with the restaurant. She's so sweet, too."

Zoey smiled, letting her mind wander. Dad was

letting José stay with Poppy until his flight to Florida. Maybe he'd let José stay indefinitely if José wanted.

"Any chance you'll stick around too next year? To be closer to Toni-Ann?" Not daring to risk eye contact, Zoey busied herself folding jeans.

"No, Zoey. You know that already. I'm going to UF. Stop trying to play dumb."

"But what about your relationship with Toni-Ann?" Zoey stopped packing and glared at José. "You'll be so far."

"I know. It sucks. We'll probably have to break up."

"What? How can you just break up with someone as nice and intelligent as Toni-Ann?" Zoey was tempted to bop her brother over the head with her laundry bag to knock some sense into him.

"I'm not *happy* about it, Zo," José said, swallowing hard. "But I just met Toni-Ann. I've been dreaming of becoming an engineer my whole life. Sometimes dreams require sacrifice. Sometimes loved ones make it hard to build a life you love . . . ," he said weakly, shooting her a pointed look.

"Including me?" Zoey asked.

"Well, you're not exactly making it easy for me with all these guilt trips," José answered honestly, sitting down in the swivel chair at her desk.

"Oh, sorry for being such a burden. At least you'll be rid of me soon," Zoey snapped, turning away from him.

José exhaled and rolled closer to Zoey in his chair.

"That's not what I mean, and you know it. I feel bad because I know you're going to miss me, but I also know that I have to go to college, and that I'll always be your big brother—no matter where I am, or what I'm doing, or who I'm dating. If I can even find anyone else worth dating after Toni-Ann," José said sadly.

Zoey said nothing, zipped her backpack closed, and began throwing more clothes into her suitcase, thinking that all the men in her family seemed to go about their dreams all wrong: Poppy about to let his business slip into foreclosure. Dad uprooting her yet again for some new job he'd probably quit within the next couple of months. José losing the girl he loved without even trying to make it work first. Zoey might not have known what her own life's dream was yet, but once she found it she was determined to find a better way to make it come true—one that didn't cause so much heartache.

13

Sunlight sparkled on Zoey's window the next morning. But she woke up tasting the garlic and rage from last night's pizza dinner. Her body felt like it had turned to concrete overnight, too, as she trudged downstairs. Finding Dad at the head of the kitchen table, wearing a new, cheerfully yellow shirt covered in emojis and poking at a plate of scrambled eggs, annoyed Zoey to no end.

"We can't head back to the city yet," he said, without looking up from his phone.

"You mean we're staying?" Zoey gasped.

"Hmm?" Dad glanced at Zoey, spotted the hope on her face, and shook his head. "No, kiddo, I just mean we can't leave till the roads are cleared. Last night's storm flooded the streets and knocked down a bunch of trees."

"Oh."

José and Poppy walked into the kitchen together.

"Thanks for coming with me, *mijo*," Poppy said.

José nodded, popping a bagel in the toaster.

"Where are you guys going?" Zoey asked, wanting to tag along. She definitely didn't want to sit in Poppy's house alone with Dad all morning.

"To see how the bowling alley handled the rain," José called from half inside the fridge.

"I'll come with you," Zoey said quickly. "I can help."

"We'll all go, Rafael. We should all help," Dad told Poppy, looking suddenly worried and standing up.

"Thank you, Michael. I'd appreciate that," Poppy said.

When Zoey saw the damage to the bowling alley, she had to work hard to hold back tears. It felt as if there was a bowling ball lodged at the back of her throat. Poppy's GONZO'S sign had lost four letters. A shutter had come loose, and a giant piece of driftwood had crashed through the bowling alley's front door in the storm, shattering the glass and letting in three inches of standing water dotted with garbage and seaweed.

"Can you still host the Summer Big Bowl Championship tomorrow?" Zoey asked Poppy.

"I don't think so, *mija*," he said, sounding as heartbroken as she felt. "You should call your friends to let them know."

"I'll just text them," Zoey said, her misery doubled. Now she had to tell Patrick, Tyler, Isa, and Lacey not only that she was moving away and couldn't be in the championship, but that they couldn't even hold it at Poppy's anymore. Zoey tried to send the text, but it wouldn't go and she realized she still didn't have any bars. "I think cell service is still down," she said.

Poppy picked up the stool behind the cash register and sat gingerly on it, looking lost. His head dropped into his hands. His shoulders shook silently for a few moments. The lump in Zoey's throat grew bigger. At last Poppy wiped his eyes. He went to help Dad and José move a big branch that had fallen outside.

The broken door creaked open. Zoey looked up in surprise to find Patrick, Tyler, and Lacey sloshing carefully through the flooded entrance.

"What are you guys doing here? Where's Isa?"

"Isa's mom wouldn't let her go out. They lost electricity in the storm, and she was worried about downed power lines in puddles," Lacey said. "Plus she needed Isa's help with the twins."

"We came to make sure Gonzo's could still host the championship," Patrick said morosely, sounding like he anticipated the worst. He kicked a piece of seaweed off his sneaker.

"Yeah, I was going to text you guys, but I still don't have service," Zoey said, waving her phone in the air and noticing that now one little bar was back. She took a deep breath and looked up at her friends. "Poppy said we can't host the championship anymore. And, uh, my dad came to pick me up last night, so I won't be able to play anyway. I'm really sorry."

"What? No! Where is he? Where's your father? I'll talk to him." Lacey craned her neck, searching for Dad. Zoey was grateful he'd already headed outside to clean up and to assess the damage on the other side of the arcade.

"I guess we should go see if the other bowling alley can hold the tournament," Patrick said, rubbing the splint on his finger. "We won't be able to play without Zoey on our team." He sighed heavily. "But I guess that's no reason for all the other teams to miss out."

"Oh, she's playing," Lacey said firmly, hooking her arm through Zoey's like she'd physically refuse to allow her to move out of state. "And the other bowling alley can't host the tournament anyway. They had way too much damage."

"How do you know?" Tyler asked. "I thought you didn't have cell phone service either."

"I stopped by on the way here. Sorry, Zo," she said, glancing at Zoey. "I just assumed Gonzo's would be in worse shape after the storm because it's on the beach. But no, a huge tree hit the generator at the other place, and they had an electrical fire. They're going to be closed for weeks, probably months. The owner was there with an insurance agent when we went to check them out."

Tyler walked over to the light switch next to the front door and flipped it. The lights flickered, but came fully on.

"At least you guys have power." He looked around. "You know, the damage here isn't *too* bad. I bet we could get this place in shape in time for the tournament. What do you think?" He looked at Zoey hopefully. Lacey and Patrick turned pleading eyes on her too.

"If the other bowling alley is out of commission, and we get a lot of people to come to the championship, then that might be the beginning of a lot more new business for Poppy. He'll get all the people to come back here who would've otherwise gone to the other place," Lacey said. "Please. We'll get everything ready for Poppy. He won't have to worry about anything." She made a shooing motion at Zoey. "Go. Convince your grandpa."

"I'll try, but no promises," Zoey said cautiously, but a spark of hope lit up her heart anyway. She headed over to Poppy, who had come back inside and was gingerly placing the wet rental shoes on thick towels to dry.

"Hey, Poppy? My friends want to help repair the damage so they can still hold the bowling championship here. The other center in town won't have power for a while. It's in worse shape than us! What do you think? They could help us fix everything!" Zoey said. Poppy didn't answer. The wet shoe in his hand seemed to consume his full attention.

"Poppy! POPPY!" Zoey waved a hand in front of his face.

"Hmm?" Poppy finally looked up, but his gaze seemed faraway.

"My friends will help us fix up Gonzo's! We can still host the tournament tomorrow and save the bowling alley!"

Poppy breathed out so hard his entire body deflated.

"*Ay, mija,* it's too late. There's no point either way. I just didn't want to worry you." He glanced back down at the wet shoe.

"What do you mean?" Zoey asked.

"I owe more on the mortgage than I can possibly make in one day from the bowling championship," Poppy admitted, looking ashamed. "It was never going to be enough. I just saw you so happy with your new friends...."

It took a moment for Poppy's words to sink in. "Oh," Zoey finally said, her voice tiny.

Dad materialized out of nowhere beside them and cleared his throat.

"Rafael, I know we've had our differences, but believe me, if anyone understands what you're going through, closing a business down, it's me," Dad said softly over Zoey's shoulder. Zoey jumped. She hadn't realized her father was even listening.

"And you're more than welcome to move with us to New York, if you want to get away and start somewhere fresh," Dad said.

Poppy looked at Dad like he'd never seen him before.

"Ah, *gracias*, Michael. I will . . . think about it," he said, and fell back onto his stool, clutching the wet shoe. He stared down at the wet floor.

Zoey couldn't take seeing Poppy this defeated, drowning in three inches of flood water.

"I forgot a few things I need in the office," she lied. "Can you help me carry them, Dad?" She didn't wait for his answer but headed down the hall to the closet with Poppy's desk and computer.

Dad followed. His eyes skimmed the bare office. Zoey noticed that Poppy had already started to take down the framed family photos that had hung on the wall behind his desk for decades. They sat in a cardboard box on his rolling chair, dusty and faded. Just like he said, Poppy had accepted losing Gonzo's before the storm, before even waiting to see whether the Summer Big Bowl Championship would magically be enough to turn things around.

"What'd you forget?"

"I'm not going to New York City with you," Zoey blurted, cutting Dad off and trying to rein in the anger and sadness running wild through her veins. She took a deep, calming breath and did her best to speak evenly.

"I don't want to move," she said, looking him earnestly in the eyes. "I have real friends for the first time, like, ever. And they're all on this bowling team, and they're counting on me to hold the summer championship at Gonzo's, and I can't let them down, and—"

"I'm sorry, Zo, but you'll make new friends next year. I've missed you while I've been gone."

"But not enough to call or text me?" Zoey shot back.

Dad scratched the back of his head uncomfortably. "I'm not a phone person, and I knew you were safe and sound with Poppy."

Once Zoey would have accepted this explanation, but now his words just sounded like an empty excuse. She inhaled deeply, focusing her thoughts.

"If you think I'm safe and sound here then why take me away?" she said. Before Dad could answer, she continued, "I *like* seeing Poppy every day. I hate moving all over the place and never feeling like I have any real friends or family, except for you and José. And I'm really, *really* sick of chasing your dreams. I've been chasing your dreams my whole life. Aren't I allowed to have some dreams of my own?" Zoey paused and saw that for once she had Dad's full attention. She thought back to what Poppy had said a few days ago about how she should take her time picking her dream. Looking at Dad's frowning face, she suddenly knew what hers was.

Taking another deep breath, she said, "Honestly, I think my dream is just to have the freedom to choose what *I* want. And right now, what I want is to stay and help Poppy hold the Summer Big Bowl Championship."

"Zoey, I know leaving is hard and I'm sorry we've had to move so much. But I really think once you get to New York City, you'll feel differently."

Any other time Zoey would have given in, but she had made up her mind—she wasn't backing down.

"You're not making José leave with you." Zoey stuck out her chin defiantly.

Dad squared his shoulders and straightened up, the way he always did with José to assert his authority. And yet, Zoey thought, Dad's military posture never won him much respect from her brother. Frankly, it wasn't doing much to earn hers, either.

"José is eighteen and heading to college soon. You're too young to decide these things for yourself. *I* am your father," Dad said, his voice more stern than before.

"Do you even have a place for us to live on our own in the city yet?" Zoey asked, crossing her arms over her chest and trying to stand as tall as she possibly could too. "Or are we just going to be crashing on couches at your friend's place?"

"I talked to him. There's a futon with your name on it," Dad said, in a tone that pitifully attempted to upgrade "futon" to "five-star hotel."

"Is his apartment in a good school district? Have you registered me for class? How long are we staying with your buddy? Am I supposed to switch schools two weeks into the school year when we move to our own place?"

Dad opened his mouth to reply, but Zoey caught him nervously jamming his hands in and out of his pockets, and she knew that meant the answers to all her questions were "no" or "I don't know." She dug in further.

"I bet there isn't enough cash in your wallet to buy a week of groceries. You've invested everything back into your job, right?" When Dad didn't say anything, Zoey went in for the kill. "If Mami were still alive, what would she think about how you're treating us?"

Dad sucked in his breath sharply like she'd just punched him. He looked away as if ashamed, and a wave of guilt and sadness washed over Zoey. She hadn't wanted to bring Mami into this, to hurt him, but she couldn't think of any other way to get through to him. When Dad looked back at her there were tears glistening at the corners of his eyes. He reached into the box and pulled out a picture of him and Mami stuffing cake into each other's mouths at their wedding. He stared at Mami with such longing that Zoey couldn't stand it anymore. She walked past her dad and marched out, back into the arcade.

She went over to Poppy. Her friends stood huddled by the entrance and flashed her hopeful thumbs-up signs. Nodding thanks for their support, Zoey slipped Poppy's wrinkly, age-spotted hand in hers and gave it a squeeze.

"Gonzo's has been your dream for too long, Poppy. We're not letting it go. At least, not yet. We're going to try to save it one last time," she said.

He stared at her for what felt like a while.

"All right, *jefa*. For you, we can try one last time," Poppy said finally. From his tone, Zoey could tell he'd agreed simply because he was too worn down to argue. But she didn't care, so long as Poppy was on board.

14

Dad left Gonzo's without saying goodbye to either Zoey or José. But Zoey was too busy to dwell on his abrupt departure. Once cell service was back, she spent the morning on the phone, calling half the members of the bowling league and their parents. Patrick called the other half. Together, they convinced everyone to come help fix up Gonzo's so that the championship could go on tomorrow as originally planned. At first, Poppy sat glassy-eyed in the corner, watching the dozens of volunteers streaming in through his broken door. But by noon, he was smiling and joking with the crowd, shouting directions and handing out soda cans and pizza slices during the informal lunch break. Zoey was relieved to see him in better spirits.

She was surprised when Eric and his team showed up to lend a hand too. They'd seemed so mean at the fancy bowling center across town, and here they were now showing such kindness. It turned out the Lightning Strikers weren't just great bowlers and steep competition, they were hard workers, too. Eric's father was a contractor and, apparently, a repair and renovations genius, and his office with all of his equipment was only a few blocks away. And Aiden, one of Eric's teammates, had a much older brother who was an IT guy for big companies. He came by after work to pitch in as well.

"Thank you so much for helping my Poppy out. It's really generous of you. I'm Zoey. What's your name again?" Zoey said to Aiden and his brother.

"I'm Zach," Aiden's brother said, jamming his phone into his pocket so fast he dropped it on the floor. Thankfully, they'd already brought in some fans and water pumps or else the phone would have been ruined by water. Zoey bent down to pick it up for him, but he snatched it brusquely out from under her.

"Um, sorry?" Zoey said, not sure what she was apologizing for, but feeling like she had to say something to fill the awkward silence that suddenly descended between them.

Zach cleared his throat. He had short, sandy hair, parted to the side, which must have been sprayed into place because not a single one moved as he talked. With his pale, nearly translucent skin, he reminded Zoey of a mannequin in the men's section of the department store where Dad had bought an interview suit last year.

"I have confidential stuff on my phone," he said.

Aiden smirked. He had straight hair parted just like his brother's, but his moved when his head nodded. "Yeah, my brother has to keep client stuff secret."

"Oh, okay," Zoey said, feeling like she was missing something.

"I'm almost done fixing the scorers," Aiden's brother said, looking past Zoey at the monitors overhead. He tapped his white slip-on sneaker on the floor. She got the impression he wanted her to leave.

"Okay, well, um, thanks again!" she said, turning to go and almost colliding with Isa. Lacey was with her too.

"Does Aiden's brother seem weird to you guys?" Zoey whispered as they walked away.

"He looked kind of cranky when he was talking to you. Like, he had frown lines on his forehead," Lacey said. "And he seemed relieved when you turned around to go."

"Right? And I was just thanking him for all his help," Zoey said. "I can't figure it out."

Isa shrugged. "The guy works with computers all day. He's probably not much of a people person. At least he's here helping, right?"

"Right," Zoey said, wondering why she had such a bad feeling about Zach. Maybe it was just that he reminded her of the month Dad worked in IT. Dad had come home complaining every day about how he couldn't be expected to take orders from millennials who had no idea what the real world was like and lived behind their phone screens ordering avocado toast.

"Stop worrying. We have a fun surprise," Isa said, rocking on the balls of her feet.

"What? I need to touch up the paint trim damaged by the flood water," Zoey said, moving in the direction of the rental counter where she'd left the paint and brushes.

"And you will, but first, we're stealing you for a minute," Lacey said. She and Isa grabbed Zoey's elbows, mumbling "shhh," and snuck out the back door. A sleek silver sedan that probably cost as much as Poppy's whole house waited in the alley outside.

"If that's the car you're kidnapping me in, then I'll go willingly," Zoey joked.

"Good. Because that's kind of what we were planning," Lacey said seriously, giving a thumbs-up to the driver, who Zoey realized was Lacey's older sister.

"What?" Zoey turned to Lacey, annoyed, and shook her arm free. "I was *kidding*. We have so much work to do before tomorrow!"

"And we're going to get it all done, we promise," Isa said soothingly, flashing Lacey a warning look. "But we realized we don't have team shirts. Now that the roads are cleared, we'll just go really fast to the mall and pick some out. We'll be back before anyone notices we're gone. And we'll have our cell phones. They'll call us if they need us." Isa waved her phone in the air.

"No. You guys go without me. I'll just wear whatever you choose—within reason," Zoey said, noticing the designer emblem on Lacey's tee and realizing she might not be able to afford a uniform selected by Lacey.

"Nooo, it won't be any fun without you. This will take, like, half an hour. Forty-five minutes max. Come on, please," Isa said, making puppy eyes.

"Yes, let's go," Lacey urged.

"Fiiine," Zoey gave in, and grudgingly climbed into the plush leather back seat of Lacey's sister's car. Remembering her promise to Poppy to keep him posted on her whereabouts, Zoey texted to let him know where she was going. She sighed as she hit send, feeling guilty for skedaddling off on a spontaneous shopping trip for herself when every second should be used on making Gonzo's sparkle. Zoey leaned back against the buttery leather headrest and listened to Isa and Lacey chatting about their favorite athletes' game day outfits in every sport from gymnastics to tennis. She sighed. For about the millionth time, Zoey wished she didn't have to worry about her family so much and could be as chill as her friends.

"Ooo, what about this one? I like the zippers on the sides. And the purple matches my favorite bowling shoes," Lacey said, picking up a plain white tee. A few unimaginative lavender stripes on the sleeves did not, in Zoey's humble opinion, warrant the thirty-five-dollar price.

"Too expensive," Zoey groaned, showing Lacey the tag. As she'd predicted, Lacey didn't seem to have a budget. And even though she'd announced she could only afford twenty bucks, that didn't stop Isa from wanting to play dress-up and try on all the clothes she couldn't afford either. Zoey tapped her foot impatiently—this was taking too long.

"How about this one?" Isa asked, holding up a collared black shirt with red color blocks that at least looked more like the search results on Zoey's phone when she'd Googled "bowling shirt."

"How much?" Zoey asked, rubbing her belly. Her stomach felt like it was full of stones. Just standing in the airy, organized portion of the juniors section was too much. The rare times Zoey had ventured into this store with Dad or José, she'd headed straight to the messy sales racks at the back and flipped through the marked-down clothes, hoping a cute top would magically appear with a price tag she could afford.

"Twelve bucks."

"Okay, let's try it on." Zoey exhaled, sighing and calculating that if they settled on that shirt she'd have about six or seven dollars in the world left to her name. But that was yet another problem that would have to wait till after the championship.

"Great! These too!" Lacey said, materializing out of nowhere with a massive armful of tops. "I didn't know what size you were, Zo," she called over her shoulder as she made a beeline toward the dressing rooms. "So I just grabbed all of them."

"Great," Zoey said glumly, following her.

The individual changing stalls didn't have mirrors. To assess their selection, shoppers had to venture outside to a giant three-paneled mirror. Lacey and Isa spun and preened in front of the mirror, but then they were also short and thin and cute—Isa in her size S or XS, Lacey comfortably sporting a size M. Towering beside them, Zoey frowned at her reflection in the mirror. The black V-neck emblazoned with sequined fireworks hung on her like a trash bag someone decorated for the Fourth of July. She glanced at the price tag poking out of her sleeve—$19.99.

Zoey grimaced. The last thing she wanted was to spend her last twenty bucks to look like a glittery garbage can.

"I think a size smaller might fit you better," Lacey said, watching her. "What do you have on now?"

"XL. I picked the same size as most of the jerseys I got from José."

"That explains it—you need different sizes depending on the cut and style of a shirt. Be right back," Isa said. She dashed back into her dressing room and emerged victoriously holding another V-neck. "Here. I grabbed an extra medium."

"No. It'll be too tight," said Zoey automatically, crossing her arms over her chest.

"Try a large then," Lacey said, handing it to her. Zoey quickly changed and when she reemerged, Lacey said, "It looks better."

"I don't know. . . ." Zoey trailed off.

"If you don't like it, we can try another shirt," Isa suggested.

"Zoey, why don't you pick something out that you might like?" Lacey offered.

Zoey looked through the pile and held up a striped shirt.

"Oh, I hate stripes," Isa said. "I think they always make my boobs look too big."

Zoey was surprised—Isa had never mentioned that she worried about her chest before.

"Well, I don't want you to wear something you won't feel good in," Zoey said. "You guys should just pick something."

"But you deserve to feel confident too!" Isa protested.

"I don't think I'll look good in anything, so it doesn't matter," Zoey said, sighing again.

"Seriously, Zo?" Lacey said, putting her hands on her hips. "There's nothing wrong with you."

"You wake up looking like a princess in a castle every day. You have no idea how hard it is to look like me!" Zoey snapped.

"Oh *puh-leaze*. Stop being such a drama queen," Lacey shot back, rolling her eyes. "You think I don't get judged all the time? I've had teachers, *teachers*, assume I was dumb just because of my style and appreciation for fashion. Also, I have a really big birthmark on my thigh that my sister used to say looked like I'd pooped myself." Lacey shrugged, and the three girls laughed.

"Okay, maybe we can agree that we all have insecurities?" Isa offered tentatively.

"Yeah," Zoey agreed. "But I still don't know if I like any of these shirts."

"Hey, I just thought of something," Isa said. "What

are the boys supposed to wear tomorrow if we buy any of these shirts for ourselves? Shouldn't we all match?"

"I hadn't thought of that," Lacey said. "We could ask the guys to wear the same color we choose. Patrick will probably want to match even if he's not playing, since he's captain."

"I guess just asking them to wear a shirt in the color that we pick could work," Isa said slowly.

"What'd you guys wear last summer?" Zoey asked.

"Patrick ordered us plain yellow shirts. They were kind of boring," Lacey said.

"Do you want to wear last summer's shirts? I can borrow Patrick's if he still has his since I'm bowling, and he can wear another one of his yellow shirts," Zoey asked hopefully. "And we can get back to work faster." She checked her watch. "It's been an hour since we left Gonzo's."

"I guess that makes sense," Lacey said, sounding disappointed.

"Perfect!" Zoey exclaimed. She hung her tops on the return rack in the hallway leading to the fitting rooms and marched out before Lacey could change her mind. "Let's go!"

The shopping trip had ended on a better note than Zoey had dared hope for, but she still felt more in her element when they came back to the welcoming scents of lane oil and cleaning supplies at Gonzo's. By midnight, they'd dried the flooded areas, touched up the paint, waxed the lanes, replaced the broken front door, and even fixed the stubborn Skee-Ball machine. Isa and her abuela Graciela wove together a festive arch with the blue and red balloons left over from the twins' last birthday party, and Tyler's mom lent them her bowling trophies and memorabilia from her past competitions to display around the alley.

By the time Zoey skipped home with Poppy and José, Gonzo's was belle of the ball, as far as bowling alleys went. Charmingly retro. Optimally situated at the boardwalk's entrance. Beautifully dressed in fresh paint and a new sign advertising tasty fare from the Triple Threat Chicken Café. Yes, they'd successfully Cinderella'd Poppy's bowling alley. Zoey drifted off to a deep sleep in a heady haze of accomplishment.

The next morning she woke at dawn to insistent knocking on Poppy's front door.

"Your friends are here!" Poppy called up the stairs.

Zoey raced down in her pajamas to find Isa and Lacey clutching bags filled with T-shirts, fabric paints, and sewing materials.

"Fashion emergency. We think we need something better than the shirts we lost in last year," Lacey said, breathlessly breezing past Zoey and dumping her bags on the couch. "Something to make us more confident."

"Seriously?" Zoey said.

"What's wrong?" asked Isa.

"I just know nothing ever looks good on me, so why waste the time trying?" Zoey said, yawning.

"This again? Come on, what are you talking about?" asked Lacey.

"Okay, you know how you're always saying that power outfits are supposed to make you feel even more confident? Well, I don't love how most clothes look on me. And I don't think I could be very confident, even if I did have a cool outfit."

"Zoey, who organized us all to fix up the bowling alley?" Lacey asked.

"What does that have to do with—"

"Just answer the question, Zo."

"Fine. Yes. I did do that."

"Exactly. And who convinced your Poppy to keep trying to save his business?" Isa chimed in.

"Me," Zoey said, smiling in embarrassment.

"Who stood up to your dad and told him you were staying here?" Lacey said.

"I did," Zoey said, looking down at her fuzzy frog slippers. She'd told Lacey and Isa about her talk with Dad on the way home from the mall yesterday.

"*Right.* Now, I don't know anyone who could have done any of those things if they didn't *already* have confidence."

Zoey had to admit they had a point, but something was still bothering her. "Yeah, I guess so. But then why don't I *feel* confident in certain clothes?"

"You just haven't spent enough time experimenting. It's like bowling—you needed to practice before you were halfway decent. You have plenty of time to figure out what 'your look' is. You don't need to rush it and have everything figured out," Lacey said.

Zoey recalled how Poppy had said the same thing about choosing a dream. She should take her time to figure things out at her own pace.

"Yeah, and what you like to wear will change, too," Isa said. "I used to hate polka dots. Until I saw this top, and then suddenly I *needed* them in my life yesterday." She stretched out the hem of her pink tee, which was covered in big black polka dots.

The girls laughed.

"Thanks, you guys," Zoey said. She dug into a nearby drawer and pulled out a pair of scissors. "Lacey, I can make that crisscross pattern you like so much on your T-shirt."

"Oh, let's do it on our three T-shirts so we match!" Isa exclaimed.

"What about the boys' shirts?" Zoey said.

"I think we can have some details that make them unique to us. But let's write CURVE BREAKERS on the front so we have some uniformity, too," Isa suggested.

"Ooo, and we can capitalize the A in 'Breakers' and add a little plus sign on top, like, because an A-plus breaks the curve," Zoey said, starting to get excited about the rainbow of fabric paints and markers Lacey was unpacking onto the old newspapers she'd spread on Poppy's dining room table.

"I love that," Lacey said, fishing out the red fabric marker.

Zoey moved the bowl of wax fruit to the top of the fridge to make room for their fashion project. "Okay, let's do this!"

Later that morning, Zoey's hands were almost too sweaty to properly grip her bowling ball. She loved the matching shirts they'd designed, but she still had butterflies in her stomach.

"I'm so nervous I think I'm going to barf," she whispered. She'd waited till Patrick was out of earshot, walking from lane to lane to shake hands with the captains of all ten competing teams.

"Don't worry. You got this. It's all math and science. Just remember your angles," Isa said, giving Zoey's hand a squeeze.

"And remember that I lost the whole thing last year after practicing for months, and a small part of Patrick will always, always hate me more than you, no matter how badly you mess up today," Tyler said cheerfully. Isa and Lacey shot him dark looks.

"If, I mean *if* you mess up," Tyler quickly backpedaled.

Isa rolled her eyes. Lacey fished out a bracelet strung together from translucent blue, green, white, and brown beads that matched Zoey's Earth Ball. "Here. You're color-coordinated now," Lacey said, winking. "I made this especially for you this morning while you were changing at Poppy's house."

"And don't forget you've got the *azabache* pinned to your shirt too," Patrick said, sneaking up behind Zoey and grinning down at the matching *azabache* pinned to his own tee.

Zoey jumped. She didn't realize Patrick had overheard.

Tyler laughed.

"C'mon man, *you* believe in good luck charms?"

"Lucky *azabaches*. Lucky jeans. Even lucky carrot sticks."

"Carrot sticks?" Isa raised an eyebrow.

"I've eaten carrot sticks before every game we've won," Patrick said. He unzipped his backpack, took out a clear, resealable plastic bag full of carrots, and began nibbling them nervously, reminding Zoey of a bunny rabbit. She burst out laughing.

"Laugh away. Last year I didn't eat carrots. You made fun of me and made me feel dumb," he said, nodding at Tyler. "And we lost at the last minute."

"What'd you snack on instead of carrots?" Zoey asked curiously.

"Graham crackers. *Tyler's* graham crackers. The graham crackers were bad luck." Patrick shook his head mournfully.

Tyler shook his own head and groaned at Zoey. "You see? You're golden next to me."

"You monster," Zoey deadpanned back. "You *cookie* monster."

Everyone burst out laughing.

Joking around with her friends relaxed Zoey. By the time it was her turn, she didn't hesitate. She marched up to that lane like she owned it (which, technically, her family did—if only for a little while longer), slid one leg behind the other, assumed proper form, and rolled her favorite Earth Ball at a perfect curve. Earth Ball had never traveled that fast or steadily when it left her hands. But today, all ten pins crashed to the ground on impact. Zoey didn't know if it was the carrots, the *azabache* on her shirt, or just all the hard work she'd put into practicing, but she let out a *whoop!* The crowd went bananas too. It was early yet, but her strike tipped the score in their favor. Patrick was so happy he picked Zoey up and swung her in a circle. And Lacey, Isa, and Tyler jumped on top of them for a group hug.

"THAT WAS AMAZING!" Lacey hollered.

"And to think you were just an itty bitty bowling baby before I taught you everything I know," Tyler teased.

Zoey's first strike ever on her first turn in the championship gave the Curve Breakers momentum. From that point on, they decimated team after team until it was down to the last two, and they found themselves head-to-head against the Lightning Strikers for the final round.

"Good luck guys," Eric called haughtily. "You're going to need it."

"Good luck yourself," Patrick shot back.

When Isa's turn came, she bowled a strike easily and mimed blowing on her nails to dry them as she pranced back to her seat. Then she bowed to the crowd before sitting down next to Zoey and leaning over to whisper, "This guy who looks like José, but way older and wearing a really tacky flamingo shirt, is standing in the back staring at us. Is that your dad?"

"Huh?" Zoey craned her neck to see where Isa was pointing. Then she spotted him. Yup, that was Dad all right. He waved when their eyes met, and beckoned for Zoey to come over to him, all the way on the other side of Gonzo's, next to the Skee-Ball machine.

Was Dad seriously planning on trying to make her leave in the middle of the championship—in the final round, no less? She wasn't going to leave, but Zoey grudgingly realized she should at least find out what Dad wanted. Luckily, the Lightning Strikers would bowl before it was her turn again.

"I'll be right back," she told Isa firmly, and slipped off the bench. Zoey gritted her teeth as she approached, staring down at Dad's sneakers until they were immediately in front of her.

"I saw that first strike, kiddo. You're really good," he said softly, surprising her.

She glanced up. Dad's eyes were red and puffy, like

he'd been crying. Zoey rocked back and forth on her feet. Her first instinct was to give him a big hug, try to make him feel better, but Zoey was still mad. She wasn't ready to hug it out and pretend nothing had happened yet. Not this time.

"Thanks," she said quietly, crossing her arms and sort of hugging herself instead. "I didn't realize you were here."

"Me and a million other people," Dad said, waving a hand at the crowd packed shoulder-to-shoulder. "I've never seen this place so full. Maybe it'll be enough to get Poppy out of the hole. If it is, it's all thanks to you, Zoey. I underestimated you."

Zoey gawked at him, processing Dad's compliment. Had he cared enough to come and watch after all? Or was he still going to try to take it all away from her—her new home and her friends and that incredible sense of really belonging somewhere for the first time in her life?

"You were right. About everything, kiddo. About me," he continued, his voice sincere. "I'm not proud of everything I've done these past few years since Mami died. But I'm going to try to make it up to you. I'm going to do my best to make things work in the city. I promise I won't give up on selling motorcycles so fast."

"Really?" she asked. Dad committing to a more stable

lifestyle sounded amazing. But she still didn't want to leave the Jersey Shore.

"Yes, and I won't make you come with me. Not yet, at least," Dad said, and Zoey could see the words pained him. "You've really bloomed here, with Poppy and your new friends. So you can stay, for now. We're going to play it by ear. Maybe you'll move in with me once I have my own place. You should know I won't be able to live without my baby for too long."

These were the exact words Zoey hadn't even realized she needed to hear from Dad right now. Her cheeks, her chin, it felt like her whole face quivered. The tension behind her eyes turned into a gathering flood. Fat tears fell onto her shiny blue bowling shoes, and she threw her arms around Dad, inhaling his familiar scent, a mix of aftershave and caramel coffee. Dad's arms circled her shoulders reassuringly, and he dropped his head to the top of hers. Zoey had spent so much of the past few weeks feeling angry and more and more distant from her father, but his hug suddenly brought her back to a thousand other hugs: When she was nervous about her first day of kindergarten the year they'd lived in Boston, begging him not to leave, and he'd hugged her goodbye, promising to bring a cannoli when he picked her up. When he picked her up that same day and she'd leaped into his arms to find a fancy white bakery box tied with pink string, as promised. When he'd pulled her and José close at Mami's funeral as they lowered her body into the ground. When he'd hugged her after sixth grade graduation, whispering he was proud into her ear.

The hug now didn't fix everything between Zoey and her dad.

But it was a good start.

As mad as she'd been at him for leaving, and maybe still was, he was her father. He'd always been there for her before, in his way. And Zoey loved him with all her heart.

When Zoey let go of Dad, she realized the top of her ponytail was wet. Dad's eyes were redder and puffier than before. He had been crying too. He sighed.

"I really wish I had the day off today," he said, looking truly sorry. "But if I'm going to try to make a real career out of selling motorcycles, then I probably need to get to work now."

"I understand," Zoey said, sniffling. "Go." She patted him on the back. "I have a bowling championship to win anyway."

Dad managed to smile, his blue eyes regaining a hint of their twinkle.

"I have no doubt you will. Call or text me later to

give me the final score. I promise I'll respond as soon as I'm able."

Zoey smiled back at him. He blinked back more tears, and glanced at something behind her head. His smile faded for a second, but then returned. Though this time it didn't reach his eyes.

"Now get back to your team. You're up next," Dad said, and gave Zoey one last hug before leaving.

Zoey took sniffling breaths all the way back to the Curve Breakers. She'd gotten what she wanted, but seeing Dad's sad expression before he'd left hurt more than she thought it would. Dazedly, she picked up Isa's fire truck red ball and, before anyone could stop her, half-heartedly rolled it down the lane. All her lessons forgotten in that instant, Zoey just chucked it like she used to before she learned proper form from her friends. The ball rolled slowly and directly into the gutter, which snapped Zoey out of her fog.

A moment of stunned silence fell over the crowd.

"I'm so sorry," Zoey said, whipping around to face her team.

Lacey and Tyler gave her sympathetic looks. Isa jumped up to give her a quick hug.

"It's okay. You can do this. Just remember . . ." Isa went on, reviewing angles and formulas and all the math and science theories as Zoey wiped at a few stray tears. She hated to cry in front of everyone.

Patrick's face was tight, but he gave her a curt nod. "It's okay. It's your dad's fault. He shouldn't have come here to mess you up on game day."

"No, he actually, um," Zoey stammered, breaking down into tears again. She wanted to say that her dad hadn't upset her this time. That she'd had the best and most honest talk she'd ever had with him. He'd actually been supportive. What was throwing her off was wondering if she was the selfish one now and should have agreed to move to the city with him immediately. But the words wouldn't come. Her shoulders slumped.

The announcer called Zoey back up for her second throw, and there wasn't more time to explain. She tried to focus, but only managed to knock down a single pin.

"Better than a gutter ball," Tyler said encouragingly when she trudged back to their bench. Patrick nodded and took a deep breath. And because everyone seemed to genuinely care, Zoey told her friends about her conversation with Dad while the Lightning Strikers took their next turn.

Lacey scrunched her nose when Zoey was done.

"You have *nothing* to feel guilty about," she said, blunt as ever. "I'd invite you to come live with me before letting you crash on the couch of some random high school friend of your dad's who you've never even met. Let your dad get it together first. He needs his own place. Then we'll talk about letting you move to New York."

Zoey half-smiled. Lacey's take was as honest and bossy as Lacey herself.

"It's great that he says he's going to try to be, like, more stable. But let him *show* you—because in the meantime, you have Poppy and us. You're in a good place right now." Isa nodded wisely. "And it sounds like your dad acknowledged that. He obviously realizes this is where you should be, or he wouldn't have let you stay. It's what *he* wants for you too, even if it hurts him to admit it."

Zoey bit her lip, letting her friends' words sink in and starting to feel better.

"I'm going to try out for baseball in the fall. I might not be able to do bowling anymore if the schedules conflict," Tyler blurted, looking at Patrick. "But if I can't make it, then you'll have Zoey as my replacement!" He turned to Zoey and winked. "Just giving you one more reason to feel good about staying, since guilt seems to work with you. Patrick's probably going to need you on the team."

Zoey smiled.

"So, no more guilt about staying, okay?" Patrick asked Zoey, in his trademark solemn tone.

"No more guilt," she said, and meant it.

"And no more gutter balls?" he added hopefully.

"Patrick!" Tyler, Lacey, and Isa shouted in unison.

"You're being very insensitive," Lacey informed him.

"No more gutter balls," Zoey agreed.

15

On her next turn, Zoey walked up to the foul line with a tightness in her belly that meant a full-blown stomachache was only one worried thought away. She felt at peace with all the Dad stuff, but the morning's winning momentum was still broken. If Zoey could choose to be anywhere in the world at that second, she'd be scarfing down a pint of cookie dough ice cream alone in her room, or kicking around a soccer ball by herself on an empty field. Instead of standing in front of all these people waiting to see if she rolled another gutter ball. Maybe even hoping that she would.

She glanced behind her and spotted José and Toni-Ann holding hands and leaning on the air hockey table. They flashed her thumbs-up signs, pumped their fists, and hollered, "Go, Zoey!" and "You got this!" She smiled at them, then heard her friends shouting "Zoey!" behind her.

Poppy joined in. Then so did her friends' parents. Pretty soon the entire bowling center was chanting her name. Everyone except the Lightning Strikers, who eyed the crowd warily and watched Zoey with sour expressions. She almost laughed out loud at Eric's reddening cheeks and the way his eyes and mouth were all drawing in toward the middle of his face, like his nose was calling them home.

Taking a deep breath, Zoey tried to tune everyone else out and focus. All she needed to think about in this moment was not rolling a gutter ball. She stared down the lane at the bowling pins so long that they started to look like tiny ghosts. Zoey blinked and squinted at them, trying to visualize a strike. Unfortunately, the image refused to come. But the pins did sort of blend together, reminding Zoey of beads on a bracelet. She thumbed the bracelet Lacey had made her for good luck. Knock one down, and the rest of the chain will follow.

She touched the *azabache* pinned to the bottom of her shirt for luck too, tucked one leg behind the other, and flung the Earth Ball with all her might. It flew down the lane, gliding with a graceful ferocity that made Zoey think of the speed skaters she'd seen compete in the last Winter Olympics. Her ball crashed straight through the pins. Eight toppled over.

Eight!

She spun around and launched into a spontaneous touchdown dance without thinking about whether she looked awkward. Then Zoey rolled a spare. Patrick jumped up from his chair in excitement. Lacey and Isa wrapped Zoey in a bear hug, and Tyler gave her a high-five.

The Curve Breakers' momentum was back.

The Lightning Strikers, though, at least as far as Zoey knew, hadn't dealt with any family crises today, and therefore, had never lost *their* momentum. They were playing best two out of three games, and, thanks to Zoey's spare and Isa's strikes, the Curve Breakers managed to win the second game. But by a single point. The third game was going to be close.

Zoey could tell Eric was worried because he got meaner with every throw.

"You hold that ball like it's a baby," Eric jeered, trying to break Tyler's concentration in the first frame. "Actually, you look like you're the baby when you hold it like that. *Wah, wah.* Poor Ty-Ty. Is your diaper wet? *Wah, wah,*" Eric mimed a crying baby, and his teammates all guffawed. Tyler's best release was his two-handed one. To Zoey's untrained eye, it *did* look like an uncoordinated toddler chucking a toy on the floor (not that she planned on telling Tyler that). But it was effective. Tyler always knocked down at least seven pins with the move.

"How is it that Eric is so nice one minute, helping us fix everything yesterday, and now he's being so mean?" Zoey whispered to Isa. "He's like two different people."

"People are complicated," Isa said. "They're not all good or all bad. They have their moments. Eric goes to our school, and I've seen him flip from cool to nasty in a second. Like, he organized a donation drive to provide turkeys to homeless families on Thanksgiving. But then, he also tried to stick Tyler's head in the toilet right before winter break."

"That's horrible! Gross. Poor Tyler," she said, eyeing Tyler as he adjusted his thick glasses, ran a hand through his messy hair, and tucked in his shirt. She hated Eric for picking on her sweet, nerdy friend.

"Poor Eric," Isa said, laughing. "Tyler's a black belt in karate and has been taking Krav Maga classes since he was five. Luckily, Eric was too embarrassed to admit Tyler walloped him, or they would've both gotten suspended. Maybe even arrested. Eric walked around with a black eye for two weeks. Haha. He hasn't tried to give anyone else a swirlie in the bathroom since. Oh look, Tyler's about to bowl."

The girls watched Tyler confidently approach the foul line.

"I'm going to pretend this ball is your head, Eric," Tyler called over his shoulder, and crouching low to

the ground, flung his ball two-handed down the lane.
Seven pins.

No one clapped. No one said anything at all. You could hear a text message pop onto the screen of a phone at the very back of the bowling alley. That's how focused everyone was on the match. The pressure turned Zoey's insides to acid, and it wasn't even her turn to bowl yet!

Tyler jumped up and down a couple of times, which Zoey had noticed was what he did when he wanted to concentrate. Then, more swiftly than she'd ever seen him move before, he picked up his ball from the return, jogged up to the approach, and sent his ball sailing one-handed down the lane. It hooked beautifully into the three remaining pins, earning a spare. Pumping his fist in the air, Tyler swaggered back to the bench. The crowd burst into cheers before quieting again.

The next Lightning Striker to bowl was Eric. He got a spare too and smirked knowingly at his teammates. Zoey wondered why he was so cocky. It was early yet and anybody's game. Her stomach was in knots.

"Are you nervous too?" she whispered to Isa.

"A little. But I feel good about our chances. It helps that we practiced here so much, thanks to you and Poppy. I know these lanes well, and that helps me calculate my angles better. The Lightning Strikers are loud and obnoxious, but they don't have the home field advantage," Isa whispered back.

"Also, I have a trick." Isa lowered her voice even further. The citrine stud in her ear twinkled like it knew her secret.

"What is it?" Zoey said, wondering for the millionth time how her friends could be so cool and sparkly under pressure. Why must she always be the one to feel anxious?

Isa looked around to make sure no one was listening.

"Okay, I pretend for a few seconds while I'm picking up my ball that the lane I'm about to approach is the red carpet before the Oscars." She closed her eyes and held up her arms. "I'm wearing a chiffon mermaid gown in a deeply stunning forest green. It has long sleeves, a high neck, an open back, and flattering ruching at the sides. All those people in the crowd, even the fans here for the Strikers, are *my* admiring fans, and I'm favorite for best actress." Isa's arms fell back down by her sides. She smiled sheepishly at Zoey. "Maybe a little delusional, but pretending I'm somewhere else makes competing more fun and less stressful."

Zoey giggled. "I thought you were going to give me a physics formula for determining the ball's velocity or something."

"The math and science are important. But sometimes—" she leaned in closer to make sure only Zoey could hear, as Tyler had just plopped down in the chair across from their bench "—I just want to dream up something fabulous," she said solemnly.

With that, she left Zoey and Tyler and sashayed to the rack to select her favorite red ball. She rolled a strike so easily that Zoey jumped about a foot in the air when she heard the pins fall heavily to the ground. The audience went wild for Isa, and Zoey laughed, picturing the throng of mostly parents and siblings watching and snapping pics on their phones from the arcade as paparazzi and photojournalists with big, professional cameras waiting to ask Isa about her Academy Award–nominated film. Indeed, when Isa spun around to find her family in the crowd, she gave them a regal wave and a smile that reminded Zoey of an actress about to be interviewed before an awards show.

When the seventh of ten frames—and Zoey's last turn to bowl for the day—arrived, the Curve Breakers were behind in points.

"Oh, it's just the new girl," Eric scoffed loudly to his teammates. "I bet she rolls another gutter ball."

"Gutter ball. Gutter ball. Gutter ball," the Lightning Strikers chanted. A few crowd members joined in.

"Seriously?" Zoey muttered, looking up in wonder to see which adults would actually boo a kid.

She spotted Eric's dad, the contractor, and Aiden's brother, standing with their hands clenched into fists, right behind the bar separating the lanes from the audience.

"Figures," she said to herself, inhaling, squaring her shoulders and scooping up her bowling ball.

"Gutter ball! Gutter ball! Gutter ball!" The chanting grew louder.

San Alejo. San Alejo. San Alejo. The Spanish words popped out of nowhere into Zoey's head. She didn't know what they meant, but remembered her mother saying them a lot as she cleaned the house to get rid of germs the year both she and José had nonstop fevers, sore throats, and runny noses. She thought it had something to do with banishing negative energy, and she made a mental note to Google the translation after the tournament.

San Alejo. San Alejo. San Alejo. Zoey heard her mother repeat it over and over in her head, and it had a calming effect on her. Her mother was here with her in spirit, she could feel it.

Zoey silently willed herself and her Earth Ball to go for the gold. She planted herself a few steps behind the foul line.

"Go, Zoey! Go, Zoey! Go, Zoey!" The Curve Breakers broke into a cheer to counter the relentless drum of "Gutter ball!"

Zoey tried to imagine the gleaming wooden lane ahead was a red carpet, like Isa, but the image didn't work for her. The idea of being a famous celebrity on TV only made her more nervous. She stared down at the brown and green swirls that conjured land masses against the sapphire blue overall hue of her bowling ball. Wisps of white paint glossed over all the other colors, reminding Zoey of the photos she'd seen in science class of Earth taken from space. The world was in her hands. She had stood up to Dad. She had convinced Poppy to host the championship. She could fling a little ball onto some wood.

Taking a deep breath, Zoey got into position and released the ball as hard as she could. It rolled right along the edge, and for a second, Zoey thought it had listened to the Lightning Strikers and planned to detour into the gutter. But no, at the last second it hooked toward the center and knocked over six pins.

Zoey exhaled and prepared to go again, musing at how the entire bowling center seemed to scream as the ball left her hands, but by some odd unspoken protocol, no one dared breathe in the pause between throws. Never mind. She used the silence to tune everyone and everything else out.

There was just Zoey and the ball in Gonzo's, *her*

family's Gonzo's. This wasn't some fancy, formal championship center, this was the happy, familiar place where she'd vacationed every summer when Mami was alive. She remembered how her mother had taught her to bowl here by placing the ball on the floor and gently rolling it off with two hands.

And with that memory in mind, Zoey rolled her ball toward the remaining pins.

And knocked them all down.

Another spare.

The majority of the crowd went wild. *Home field advantage indeed,* Zoey thought contentedly, remembering Isa's words as she trotted victoriously back to her team, expecting them to congratulate her.

Instead, they were all staring up at the monitor above their heads with grouchy expressions. Zoey's stomach plummeted to the floor. Oh no. She'd messed up. Maybe if she'd pretended she was on the Oscars red carpet she would have bowled a strike. And she needed that prize money to help Poppy. Every little bit counted. Why had she been thinking all that nonsense about holding the world in her hands?

"I'm so sorry. I really tried my best," Zoey said, trying to look each of her teammates in the eye. But none of them would meet her gaze.

"What?" Lacey said, turning toward her.

"I'm so sorry that I didn't roll a strike. I know you guys were counting on me to put in my absolute best performance, and I only made a spare. But I thought that wasn't so bad, you know?"

"We're not mad at you," Lacey said.

"Oh. Then what's wrong? Why does everyone look so mad? And what is Patrick writing?" He was scribbling furiously on a piece of paper, while Tyler pressed buttons on his phone with equal furor.

"They're adding up our score. Isa did the math in her head. Patrick's doing it now by hand, and Tyler's using the calculator on his phone. The scorer isn't marking enough points for our spares."

"What?"

"Isa caught the glitch because she'd been keeping track of the score in her head—and she glanced up at the monitor a couple of minutes ago and realized we're two points behind where we should be, before counting your spare. And we've had exactly two spares before yours."

Tyler looked up grimly. "Isa's math is right."

Patrick stood up and beckoned to the Lightning Strikers.

"Eric, we need a time-out."

"Why? You want to forfeit? Getting cold feet because you know you're going to lose?" Eric snickered.

"No. There's a problem with the computer. It's not counting spares right."

"Oh yeah?" Eric asked, a shadow passing over his face. His tone sounded a little too innocent to Zoey's ears.

"You guys had a spare a few frames ago too. Did it count yours correctly?" Zoey asked, suddenly suspicious.

Isa glanced up at the scoreboard and did the math ridiculously fast in her head.

"It did," she said, putting her hands on her hips.

"So the glitch is only happening on our score?" Tyler asked.

"Your score looks fine to me. Don't be sour losers," Eric said, shrugging them off.

"The expression is 'sore losers,'" Isa retorted.

Eric rolled his eyes at her. "Okay, genius, whatever you say."

"If you think I'm a genius, then why don't you trust my math?" Isa shot back.

Aiden walked up to the group huddled around the ball return between their two lanes before Eric could answer. "What's going on?" he asked.

"Nothing," Eric said. "We're going to keep playing."

"I want Mr. Martin to check it out," Patrick said.

"I thought Mr. Martin was dead?" Zoey whispered to Lacey.

"The one they're talking about is his son, who took over running the championship when his dad died last year. He's over there," Lacey said, inclining her head. Zoey glanced at where Lacey was pointing and spotted a man with sparse silver hair who looked to be about a hundred years old himself, dozing in a folding chair in the corner of the alley.

"Him?" Zoey asked, her stomach tying itself back into the knot that had finally come untangled after the pressure of her last turn was over.

"Yup. Technically, he's in charge. This summer tournament is totally independent of other leagues and tournaments. Mr. Martin Senior—the dead one—wanted to do his own thing without worrying about official league guidelines and stuff. Like, there are no appeals or higher authorities, or even line judges because of the sensor. Everything is done by computer, and the only human with any real power to decide something like whether there was cheating is Mr. Martin Junior," Lacey explained. "It's not looking good for us," she finished worriedly.

Zoey frowned and tuned back to the conversation Patrick and the others were having with Eric and Aiden.

"If you go bother Mr. Martin about this, then my dad's going to have to send Zoey's grandpa a big bill for all the free work he put into this place yesterday. I heard him complaining this morning about how much the time cost him," Eric said.

"*What?* That's not fair! It was understood that everyone was volunteering for free so that we could hold the championship here today like we originally planned!" Zoey was incensed. "Plus, it's not like your dad bought any special supplies. He just used the tools he already had to help fix stuff!"

"Yeah, but he's a contractor. He didn't sign anything agreeing that he didn't expect to be paid. Poppy accepted the labor. At least a few hundred dollars' worth, maybe even a few thousand. My dad's a *high-end* contractor. He did some work recently for Lacey's parents. Enjoying that shiny new kitchen? Maybe you could make me some cookies." Eric winked at Lacey, who scowled back at him. She balled her fists, and Zoey could tell she wanted nothing more than to punch Eric in the face.

Lacey wasn't the only one. Zoey dug her own fists deep into the pockets of her jeans.

"I am *not* baking *you* cookies!" Lacey spit.

Eric and Aiden laughed. The crowd was starting to get restless. A few people called out, demanding that someone take their turn. Poppy suddenly appeared at Zoey's side.

"What's going on? Why you stop playing?" he asked.

"Was the scoreboard damaged at all during the storm?" Lacey asked him.

"No, I don't think so. I don't see anyone touch it."

"Dylan, go bowl," Eric barked at one of his teammates. Poppy headed back to the audience.

Suddenly, Zoey remembered seeing Zach at the scoreboard yesterday. How strange he'd been about his phone. She turned to Aiden and glared. "Your brother rigged the scorer when he was 'fixing' it, didn't he?" she said, making air quotes.

Eric smirked. "I don't know what you're talking about." But Zoey noticed Aiden carefully watching Eric's reaction and tapping his foot restlessly on the floor.

"Don't be jealous just because we're great bowlers," Aiden said, but there was no bite to his words. He looked nervous to Zoey.

"You're not great bowlers. You're great cheaters!"

More people were booing now, yelling for them to get going. Patrick still hadn't called an official time-out, and Dylan had just started the next frame on a strike. It was Lacey's turn next, and the Curve Breakers had to decide whether to let her bowl or go wake up Mr. Martin and accuse the Lightning Strikers of cheating.

Zoey could tell her teammates were clamoring for

justice, but she had to protect Poppy. If Eric made good on his threat, her Poppy would be in even more debt. The whole point of holding the championship at Gonzo's was to save it, not to put Poppy's balance sheet further in the red.

"Give us a second," she told Eric and Aiden, turning her back and motioning for the Curve Breakers to huddle alone for a second in their lane.

"I can't risk putting Poppy more in debt. I'm really sorry, guys," she said.

"Eric's just bluffing. Everybody knew they were volunteering their time for free yesterday," Tyler scoffed, but Lacey looked worried.

"I don't know. I think everyone should have known, but we didn't, like, make a big announcement, 'Hey, everyone! You're working for free!' And hiring a contractor can be really expensive, and Eric's dad did get kind of aggressive when he put in the wrong sink and my parents refused to pay until he put in the right one. They worked it out eventually, but it was a headache, and my mom swore she would never hire his company again."

"But they're cheating!" Isa said, looking like she wanted to burst into tears. Zoey wanted to cry too. She felt like she was selfishly forcing her friends to give in to a bully's blackmail. They might lose the championship they'd worked so hard for. But it was her friends or Poppy. "Dreams require sacrifice," José had said. Man, was he right, Zoey thought. It sure sucked though.

Patrick seemed to shrink to half his height, but shuffling his feet and staring down at his broken finger, he sighed and said, "It's only two points, guys. Poppy's been really good to us. He gives us a huge discount every time we bowl, and we wouldn't even be able to compete today if he hadn't let us basically take over Gonzo's yesterday. I don't want him to have any trouble with that awful family."

"You're right," Tyler agreed. "Besides, we're good enough to win this even without those two points."

"Yeah. How mad will they be when they can't even beat us by cheating? You got this, Lacey," Zoey said encouragingly.

"Cookies," she muttered. "I'll show that jerk where he can go buy cookies," Lacy said through gritted teeth.

With his back as straight as an arrow, Patrick marched confidently over to Eric and the rest of the Lightning Strikers.

"We've decided not to request a time-out to challenge technical difficulties. But if the scoreboard doesn't count Zoey's last spare correctly for the seventh frame, I *will* personally tell Mr. Martin, and everybody here, that you guys are big, stinking cheaters, even if that means forfeiting the championship," Patrick warned.

Eric shrugged coolly. "I still don't know what you're talking about," he said, but Zoey noticed Aiden slipping his phone out of his pocket and frantically tapping the screen. Hmm. Zoey bet his brother had given him an app or something to control the scorer. Unlocking her own phone, Zoey typed herself a quick reminder to tell Poppy to have the scorers fixed after the championship.

Fueled by rage, her face pinker than Poppy's beet juice jar, Lacey grabbed her favorite purple ball from the ball return and hurled it down the lane.

A strike!

The Curve Breakers were all too angry at the Lightning Strikers to cheer, offering Lacey grimly determined high-fives as she stomped back to the bench. But the audience filled in with a rousing round of applause that buoyed their spirits. Zoey glared at Eric, who looked a little shaken as he glanced up wide-eyed at the scoreboard.

"Look at Eric's face. He underestimated you," Zoey said, nudging Lacey.

"I know! That strike felt *amazing*! And I didn't even remember to match the ball to my outfit today. I think that's my first ever mismatched strike," Lacey mused earnestly.

Zoey giggled. Some of the tension evaporated from her

back, and she let herself relax against her cold metal seat.

"Oh look," she said, pointing at the lane beside theirs. "Aiden's turn."

Lacey stood up and edged as close as she could get away with to the Lightning Strikers.

"Cheater!" she coughed.

"Cheater!" coughed Tyler, standing up next to her.

"Cheater!" coughed Zoey and Patrick, chiming in.

All that fake coughing must have psyched Aiden out, because he rolled his first gutter ball of the game. It also woke Mr. Martin, who tottered over on his cane.

"Are you kids feeling all right? There's been a summer flu going around," he asked, sounding genuinely concerned.

Zoey cleared her throat.

"I feel okay. My throat's, uh, just scratchy from all that cheering," she said quickly.

"Yeah, we'll drink something," Isa said, holding up her water bottle and trying hard not to laugh.

Smirking at how frazzled the Curve Breakers got trying to cover for taunting him, Aiden knocked over five pins on his second throw. Tyler bowled next. Nine pins. That tied the score. Though, since the Lightning Strikers had cheated, the Curve Breakers *should've* been ahead by two points, thought Zoey darkly.

It all came down to Isa and Eric in the tenth and final frame. It was Eric's turn first. He lumbered over to the rack between their lanes to pick up a sleek black ball that reminded Zoey of a giant Magic 8-Ball. She walked up to him.

"I heard you delivered turkeys to families in need for Thanksgiving."

He glanced down at her, his eyebrows furrowing together to form one long, fuzzy pipe cleaner. "Yeah. So?"

"So inside of this," Zoey said, waving from his head to his toes, "there's a person who's not *always* awful. Who knows you did the wrong thing cheating, and then trying to blackmail me with my grandfather."

"You saying you want to go get Mr. Martin and accuse me of something?" Eric asked. Zoey could tell he was trying to sound tough, but his voice had lost its menace. He sounded nervous. Maybe even a touch guilty. His usually icy blue eyes had gone cloudy.

"No. I'm saying if you win this, we both know you won't *really* have won," she said. "And it won't feel good. Even if you keep putting on a show."

With that, Zoey spun on her heel and went back to the bench, leaving Eric to gawk after her.

"What'd you tell Eric? He looks like you threatened to have Tyler unleash his Krav Maga skills on him again," Isa said, glancing at Eric's hunched shoulders as he trudged to the foul line.

"Hey, Eric! You look like your dog just died," Lacey teased. "Want me to bake you some cookies?" His shoulders slumped even further. She turned to Zoey. "Seriously, what'd you tell him? It's like you deflated Frankenstein."

"I just gave him a little guilt trip," Zoey said, her cheeks going rosy in both embarrassment and delight. "He deserved it!"

"Oh, he totally deserved it," Lacey agreed.

They watched Eric sigh and roll a gutter ball.

Patrick's eyes widened. "We've been bowling against Eric for two years, and I've *never* seen him get a gutter ball. Wow, I guess Zoey's our secret weapon."

Zoey shook her head. "The secret weapon is Eric's own conscience. If he weren't playing dirty, I would have never called him out on it."

Beside them, the Lightning Strikers shifted uneasily, and it felt like the entire bowling alley held its breath to see what Eric would do next. Watching him reminded Zoey of a wounded lion, stripped of his pride.

"Do you think he threw that gutter ball on purpose? Like, does he want to lose now because he feels too guilty?" Zoey wondered. The idea of the Lightning Strikers throwing the game at the very end was so . . . unsatisfying.

"Nah, that's not Eric's style," Isa said appraisingly. "I think you just killed his focus."

"Oh," Zoey said, feeling simultaneously guilty and also angry at herself for feeling bad when Eric was the one who had cheated and rightfully deserved to be off his game.

"Time out!" called Aiden. He and his teammates huddled around Eric. Zoey couldn't hear, but she thought they were giving him a pep talk because Eric stood up straighter when he emerged for his second roll.

Careful not to look at any of the Curve Breakers, Eric picked up his ball from the return, jogged more determinedly up the approach, and knocked over five pins.

Six pins. We just need six pins, Zoey thought.

Isa was up next, and she practically bowled strikes in her sleep, Zoey thought excitedly. The game was theirs.

"Don't get cocky," Patrick said worriedly to Isa, who waved him off.

"I got this," she said, and planted a kiss on her lipstick red ball before sashaying up her imaginary red carpet to bowl what would surely be a strike.

But just as Isa released the ball, Aiden sneezed. A huge, phlegmy, foot-stomping sneeze that reverberated in the pin-drop silence of the bowling center and sent Isa's throw askew. Her ball landed in the gutter.

"You did that on purpose!" she shouted, spinning around angrily to confront Aiden. The Lightning Strikers snickered. Aiden held up his hands innocently.

"When you have to sneeze, you have to sneeze."

"That was *obviously* a fake sneeze meant to distract Isa," Lacey accused, going nose-to-nose with Aiden.

"I don't know what you're talking about. All that coughing earlier over on your side. I think there must be a bug going around, like Mr. Martin said." Aiden cleared his throat, making little coughing sounds. "Yup, I'm definitely coming down with something."

Isa glared at him.

"Ignore them," Zoey said, turning her back on the Lightning Strikers. "You are the beautiful favorite for best actress at the Academy Awards, remember?"

Isa nodded, her eyebrows furrowed with determination. She picked up the ball, and just as she was about to release it, Aiden sneezed again. Isa's hand shook slightly as the ball flew from her fingers. It landed with an awkward thud, and rolled down the center of the lane at a snail's pace.

Lacey pulled at her ponytail. "Ahhh, how is this happening in slow motion?"

Beside her, Patrick put his hands on his face and peeked out from parted fingers like he was watching the scariest part of a horror film.

Finally, Isa's ball reached the end of its journey, not so much crashing into as nudging seven pins out of its way.

Seven pins!

"We won!" Patrick hollered, dropping his hands from his face. "We won! We really won!"

"We won!" Lacey echoed, then Zoey, Tyler, and Isa. They came together in a big, jumping, bear hug that grew bigger as their families rushed forward to pile on.

Mr. Martin hobbled over to place a gold medal around each team member's neck—which Isa informed Zoey contained delicious milk chocolate inside. He also announced the grand prize would be divided equally between the team members and set aside as scholarships for college. Zoey was a little bummed she couldn't use the cash now, like she'd originally thought, but she knew José would be proud that she had earned a little something toward college. Mr. Martin handed each Curve Breaker a small metal trophy and the entire bowling alley erupted in cheers, hoots, and hollers.

"Who are all these people?" Zoey whispered to Lacey, suddenly realizing the crowd had tripled in size.

"The other teams' families. Random people from the boardwalk who just wanted to see what all the fuss was about, like, why people were streaming in here by the dozen. Oh, and my mom invited a ton of people—the

PTA, her book club, Pilates class, yoga class, rowing class, like, basically her whole gym, plus everyone at her office and beauty salon. Patrick's dad invited all their cousins. Apparently, he has, like, a million cousins. Oh, and Tyler's mom brought some of her professional bowling friends. They said they might come back to bowl for fun here once in a while."

Zoey grinned. Patrick grabbed the whole group into another bear hug. She'd never seen him happier. He may as well have won the state lottery.

"Never mock my carrots again," he told Tyler.

Zoey swelled with pride and was glad to see some of the people heading to the arcade games and the shoe rental counter, where José was renting out shoes and balls for games. Her plan had worked! Gonzo's was so much busier today than she'd ever seen it! She turned to find Poppy in the crowd. But he wasn't there. Then she spotted him by the door, shaking hands and smiling at Mr. Silos. *Oh no.*

16

Zoey ran over to Poppy to try to stop him from doing anything drastic. But she was too late. Mr. Silos slipped out the door just as Zoey reached Poppy's side.

"Did you just agree to sell Gonzo's?" she panted, clutching a stitch of pain in her side.

"Yes, but not to Mr. Silos. I just told him 'no' for the last time." Poppy smiled mysteriously.

"Huh?" Zoey was confused.

"Thanks to you, my little *jefa*, and to all the beautiful repairs and improvements you got your friends to make because you never, ever give up on me, I got another offer—a much better offer—from Mr. Fulco, who owns the other bowling alley across town—the one that's going to be closed for a while because of the electrical problems. Gonzo's will become another location under the Fulco brand, but I'm going to stay working here as the manager."

"But can't you give it a few more days? To see if the buzz from today keeps bringing in a lot more business? Like, maybe we'll still be packed tonight and all day tomorrow. . . ." Zoey stopped talking because Poppy was shaking his head "no."

The rush of being part of the winning team dissolved into the air around them. Zoey's shoulders slumped. Who cared if Mr. Martin's son was going to give each member of the Curve Breakers a four-hundred-dollar scholarship? Zoey had lost what really mattered. And she couldn't even offer Poppy her share of the grand prize because it turned out the cash had to be saved for college.

"I'm so sorry, Poppy," she said, trying not to cry. "I wanted to save Gonzo's for you."

"But you did, *mija*! This is the best of both worlds. I told you, I stay working for the bowling center. I just not going to have the headache of owning it anymore. And I never get this offer if not for you and your friends and José fixing all the machines and making everything so beautiful again. Maybe even more beautiful than before," Poppy said, glancing up appreciatively at the stars Zoey and Lacey had glued to the ceiling.

"Oh," Zoey said, processing Poppy's words slowly.

"So, this is, um, good news? Even though you won't own Gonzo's anymore, and it won't be your name on the sign?"

"Yes, *mija*. Very happy. Your Poppy getting old, getting close to retirement, and I don't need the headache of owning anymore. Now I get to keep doing the job I love, and just worry about earning a salary."

After a moment, Zoey nodded, remembering how Dad always said dreams needed the freedom to grow and change. Owning the bowling alley was Poppy's original dream. And he'd done it for decades. Now that he'd entered another stage of life, it was time for the dream to change.

"And now I will have more time to spend with you. To watch your bowling games. But didn't you also say something about trying out for soccer in the fall?" Poppy said.

"I did. Maybe I can do both?" Zoey said, relieved she didn't have to worry about Mr. Silos destroying her family's business anymore, and excited about the year ahead.

That night, Zoey twirled in front of Mami's dresser mirror. The yellow eyelet dress Lacey had lent her for the team's celebratory dinner flared nicely. A few too many ruffles, Zoey thought, running the fingernails she'd painted lilac over the ruffled sleeves and hem. Still, Zoey twirled and realized she thought the girl twirling back in the mirror looked beautiful—because Zoey *felt* amazing. She had stepped outside her comfort zone and learned to bowl and made new friends. She'd won a championship and helped save an updated version of her grandfather's dream. After accomplishing all that, Zoey knew now for sure that she could tackle her own dreams and see them through. And for once, she wasn't worrying about whether or not she was *enough*—capable enough or girly enough or even Latinx enough. She wasn't worried about Gonzo's or her dad or even José going off to college. She was happy just being herself, here, in this moment.

"Zo!" Zoey turned and saw José gaping at her.

"You look—" José's voice broke and he faltered.

"What?" Zoey asked, concerned.

"You just . . . for a second, you looked like Mami," José said, smiling. He bit his lip and jammed his hands into his jeans pockets, leaning against the doorway.

"Oh." Zoey glanced down at the makeup she'd picked up that afternoon at the drugstore and then up at the mirror again, trying to see the resemblance. Dad had left twenty bucks with José to give to Zoey to buy herself a treat—anything she wanted. And she'd finally splurged on some makeup of her very own. Dark blue eyeliner to trace on both her upper and lower lash lines and peach lip gloss because it had been her mom's favorite color to wear. She'd also taken down her ponytail, blow-dried her hair, and combed it to the side like Mami used to. But her mouth was thinner and her nose was bigger than her mother's had been. Still, there was a resemblance to her mother that she'd never noticed before, and glimpsing it made Zoey super happy.

"Thanks."

José took a few steps into the room and fiddled with their mother's childhood collection of Precious Moments figurines sitting atop the dresser. He stared at the floor like he was thinking about something else.

"What's wrong?"

José shrugged.

"I know something's wrong. Tell me," Zoey said, worried.

"I'm okay. Enjoy your dinner. You deserve it," José said, turning to go.

"No! I can't go knowing there's something wrong. I'll be wondering what it is all night. Just tell me."

José spun around. "I just, I guess I miss Mami a lot sometimes," he said, glancing at the pictures of their mom when she was a kid still taped to the dresser.

"Yeah," Zoey said, suspecting that wasn't all that was bugging her brother. "What do you miss specifically?"

"Everything," he said, exhaling.

Zoey waited for him to elaborate. He sighed.

"I just wish I could get Mami's opinion about girl stuff. I don't have any women to talk to," José said finally.

"You wish you knew what Mami would tell you to do about Toni-Ann, like whether to break up, because you're falling in love with her. Am I right?"

José raised an eyebrow at her. "How'd you know?"

"It's obvious, duh," Zoey said.

José grimaced.

"Yeah, I am. But I leave for school in just a few weeks. And I can't give up college. No way. I also don't want to break up. But have we even been dating long enough to try long distance?" José ran a hand through his hair.

"Yes," Zoey said simply.

José looked at her and laughed.

"It's not that easy, Zo. Long distance is ridiculously hard. What if she breaks my heart, and I end up too depressed to study enough to keep my scholarships? I've been working to be an engineer, like, my whole life. I can't get distracted now by some girl. Except that—"

"She's not just some girl," Zoey finished for José. "She's Toni-Ann."

"Right." José took a deep breath.

"Still sounds like an easy decision to me," Zoey said,

studying her new mascara and wondering whether to try some on for the first time, but hesitating. If she messed up the mascara it might mess up the rest of her eye makeup too.

"Can I tell you a secret?"

"Of course," Zoey said, breaking the mascara out of its packaging and feeling just the tiniest bit of a thrill.

"I'm afraid of being like Dad," José whispered. "You know? Jumping from one thing to another all the time. Chasing a million different things, and never committing long enough to make a success out of any one dream."

"Oh, I know. Same here," Zoey said, feeling lighter as she admitted the words out loud to the only other person who'd grown up with Dad and could really understand. "But we're not Dad. We're our own people. And we're allowed to have more than one dream at a time."

Zoey remembered how she'd once thought she couldn't be girly if she liked sports or didn't know fashion, or how she'd worried she was too American or second-generation to be Cuban at the same time. But Isa had been right—why couldn't she or José be all the things?

"You're allowed to go to college *and* have a girlfriend." Zoey smiled, opening the mascara tube and examining the wand.

Trying not to smear it, she brought the wand up to

her eyes but barely touched it to her lashes. Then grew braver and brushed on a bit more. She studied her handiwork in the mirror. Wow. A little mascara went a long way. Her lashes were suddenly thick and long. So much so that she became aware of their presence: A black fringe suddenly curtained the top of her sightline. Zoey blinked a couple of times. Wearing mascara might take some getting used to.

José smiled back. "I'm no expert. But you're doing a pretty good job with the makeup."

"Thanks." Zoey was inordinately proud she hadn't smudged on her first go-round. Though she wasn't sure if she'd make mascara a regular part of her makeup routine. Unless she could figure out a way to apply it without obstructing her vision. She made a mental note to ask Lacey and Isa for tips, then reflected on how much had changed so fast. Before moving to the Jersey Shore, she hadn't had any other girls in her life she could talk to about this stuff.

"Thanks for the advice, too," José said. "What am I going to do in college without your sage counsel?"

"Ah, but you need not go without, *mi hermano*. Call me. Text me. Video message me. There are so many ways to keep in touch," Zoey said.

"Fair enough. But you promise to do the same too,

okay? Keep me in the loop on Gonzo's and go visit Toni-Ann once in a while. Make sure she's thinking of me."

"Definitely. Gonzo's will be named Fulco's though. And remember you're coming back to visit here too. Thanksgiving. Winter break. Spring break. Not just Toni-Ann. You have to come back and visit *me* too. You know—your totally awesome *hermanita* who's full of the good advice?"

"I will. I promise. Aw, come here, Zo." José pulled Zoey into a great big hug and rested his chin on her dark brown hair.

"Hmm. It appears I'm going to miss my little sister more than I thought when I go to college."

Zoey smiled into José's navy polo shirt. She'd spent so much of the summer feeling like she was going to be miserable missing José when he went to school, while he wouldn't miss her at all. Now she knew the missing would go both ways—what a relief. Plus, she'd made friends. And he'd met Toni-Ann. For once, the Finolio siblings weren't all alone. They'd both found more people to care about this summer. People who genuinely cared about them back.

"I'll miss you too. But we're going to be okay," Zoey said, realizing that for the first time, maybe ever, she was the one reassuring José instead of the other way round.

So she said the words again, believing them.

"We're going to be okay."

ACKNOWLEDGMENTS

First and foremost, eternal thanks to my brilliant editor, Catherine Laudone, whose insightful vision and beautiful editing truly made *The Dream Weaver*. I am so grateful to be on your team.

To my amazing agent, Rebecca Podos: Thank you so much for being the first person in publishing to believe in me as an author, and for your steadfast faith and support. I'm so grateful I get to work with you, and eternally thankful to DVpit for connecting us.

A million thanks to everybody at Simon & Schuster: Beth Adelman—copyeditor, Hilary Zarycky—interior designer, Jenica Nasworthy—managing editor, Martha Hanson—production manager, Shivani Annirood and Milena Giunco—publicists, and Justin Chanda—publisher.

Extra-special thanks to Lucy Ruth Cummins for designing such a stunning cover and to Elizabeth Stewart for the gorgeous illustrations.

Thank you, Alaina Lavoie, JoAnn Yao, and We Need Diverse Books for a lovely cover reveal on social media and allowing me to guest blog, and also for all the incredible work WNDB does to support diverse authors.

To Las Musas, I'm incredibly humbled and grateful to be part of this talented group of exceptional and brilliant writers. Thank you so much for the thousand ways you all inspire me with your stories, humor, and strength.

To my mom, thank you for taking me to the library all those weekends when I was a kid to check out piles upon piles of books.

To my husband and children and our entire family, I love you all more than words can say. Thank you for everything.

To all the kids and kids at heart who pick up this story, thank you from the bottom of my heart for reading. I hope all your dreams come true soon and bring every happiness when they do!